21ˢᵀ CENTURY
AFFAIRS

Published by Penciled In
5319 Barrenda Avenue
Atascadero, CA 93422
penciledin.com

ISBN-13:   978-1-939502-43-8

Cover photography
    by Alexander Krivitskiy
    provided by Unsplash

Book and cover design
    by Benjamin Daniel Lawless

21ST CENTURY AFFAIRS

BY
ANDY GREENSFELDER

OTHER BOOKS BY ANDY GREENSFELDER

Drop Dead Art

A Life of Stories: Family, Friends and Experiences

To Jeanie and our 48-year affair.

CHAPTER 1

The receptionist behind bullet-proof glass buzzed George Roth into the Family Planning Center. Down the hall on the second floor, Sheila Szabo, George's fundraising co-chairperson, sat alone in the board room. She wore a sleeveless white tennis outfit, and her somewhat tousled, gray-sprinkled black hair suggested she had come from a match. Walking across the room, he caught the scent of dry sweat he liked on Bonnie when she jogged. Before either he or Sheila, a new Board member whom he hardly knew, spoke he looked forward to working with her.

She rose and held out her hand. "I hope you don't mind my getting started."

"Glad you did. Sorry I'm late."

"I didn't realize we get to be so nosy." She pointed to a computer printout that contained information on prior donors. "There's all kinds of fun stuff here."

"Oh?" George said.

"Look at this. Would you believe Mrs. Gotchold gave five thousand dollars last year? She comes to board meetings in those dresses that look like she bought them a couple of centuries ago."

George smiled and relaxed even though he was somewhat taken aback by Sheila's irreverence. Although she had come on the board only last September, the board president thought enough of her to make her fundraising co-chairperson. She didn't strike him as catty—more like a little girl tripping through her mother's desk.

"And Mr. Springer…" she started to laugh. Not a chuckle that built with the humor, but a free, unrestrained laugh, like an Olympic champion at almost-full speed out of the starting blocks. George looked over his shoulder to see if someone might hear. The chipped plaster walls were painted institutional yellow that always reminded him of his first-grade class room.

Sheila's laugh stopped as suddenly as it had started, and with a mischievous smile, she thrust the printout at George. "Look at this." MR. SPRINGER DONATES SEVERAL GROSS OF ASSORTED CONDOMS. DO NOT ASK FOR MONEY BECAUSE IT MAKES HIM THINK WE DON'T APPRECIATE HIS RUBBERS.

"What do you think "assorted" means?" Sheila said. "You see condoms sitting out in drug stores these days. I've always marveled at the different colors and ribbings and lubrications. Or does it mean small, medium, large?"

George also laughed, a little louder and freer than usual. They had just sat down together. Could she be coming on to him? He looked at her. They both smiled. Bonnie said he was so naive about women that one could have her hand in his fly for several minutes before he realized she wasn't trying to mend his zipper.

No, it wasn't a come-on. It was like Sheila's tongue was grafted to her mind. He envied her. A super censor, like a filter, sat between his thoughts and his lips.

"Maybe we can give our volunteer solicitors a tour of the clinic one of these days, and Mr. Springer can tell us what assorted means," George said. "How do you think we should divvy up these names?"

"Hey, that's a wonderful idea," Sheila said. "All our solicitors should tour the clinic. Make them better fund raisers. This is fabulous. We've only just begun and you've figured out the kickoff."

The door swung open and Seri McQuade, the agency's executive director, looked in. "Let's go. We've got bomb threat." Quickly, they walked around the tables, Sheila throwing her navy blue trench coat over the tennis dress, as they followed Seri.

Down the hall at the top of the stairs, they waited in front of the clinic while patients and staff, single file, walked past. The board had discussed how to deal with threats, but George had never been here during one. He pictured an explosion, bits of plaster walls flying across the corridor. Bodies on the floor amidst the reek of gun-powder. Others must be having similar thoughts, but no one panicked.

The restrained, organized evacuation of the clinic confirmed what George already knew from staff reports given at board meetings. The agency went through this routine far too often following bomb threats, sometimes several times a week. Seri, Sheila and George were the last to leave and passed two firemen and a policeman coming up the stairs.

On the sidewalk, George asked, "Did anyone claim responsibility?"

"Friends of God," Seri said. "Not an organization anyone knows. No one ever shows their face in these things."

"Whom do you suspect?"

"SAVE or one of their crazy members."

"Sanctimonious bastards," George said. SAVE, the militant anti-abortion group, harassed and sometimes terrorized patients outside the clinic. Three or four of them would descend on an arriving woman, often a teenager, shove pamphlets in her face, cajole her to keep her "baby." They'd kneel and pray as the patient tried to get to the door, and threaten her with God's retribution. George wished that the number of people killed in the name of God were as few as the number of abortions.

"You sure you want to do that debate?" Seri asked.

"More than ever." For years George had tried to arrange an abortion debate. But the Opposition preferred street demonstrations to logical discussion. In the past year SAVE members had blocked entry to three abortion clinics, and Susan Cordry, their leader, had spent two weeks in jail. Then a month ago, KQQV had invited SAVE and the Family Planning Center to send representatives for an hour on the radio. Seri had asked George because he was chair of the agency's speaker's bureau. Neither had expected SAVE to accept the invitation, but they did.

"Sorry to inconvenience you," Seri said. "This will take a while."

"Let's plug our parking meters," Sheila said.

George and Sheila headed up Delmar, the same Delmar that the comedian, Dick Gregory, said was the longest street in the world, running from Africa to Israel. in this area an inner city street with store fronts on both sides. One shop, closed for months, looked like it had been looted, mannequins in disarray, some without arms or legs, some in underwear or half-naked. One on the floor had what looked like a bullet hole in her chest. They passed a resell it shop with a scuffed black and white tile floor, full of people sorting through loaded bins. Then an antique shop jammed with so much junk that the owner emptied furniture onto the sidewalk each morning to clear room inside for customers.

"This bomb stuff is scary," Sheila said. "I wouldn't want my daughter exposed to it."

"How old is your daughter?"

"Debbie's sixteen. Actually the clinic's safer than an evening with her adolescent male friends." She gave a short laugh.

"My daughter knew more about sex than she knew about boys," George said, recalling the Center's pamphlets he used to bring home. He still felt relieved that Robin had survived her wild teens without becoming pregnant.

"I tell Debbie about hormones and heat," Sheila said with such emphasis on heat that George caught himself leaning away.

"Hormones and heat?"

"You were a teenage boy. Girls need to hear how their big strong daddies, with everything under control, couldn't keep it in their pants when they were sixteen.

At 50 George had grown up before younger people had learned to talk more freely about sex. While a little uneasy about Sheila's language, he envied her openness. She had it right, though he couldn't imagine having told Robin about his teenage desire for sex.

"That's the truth, isn't it?" she said as she put her hand on his arm. Speechless, he turned, and that's when she laughed. Loud and raucous as she grabbed him and pulled him along. "You don't have to answer, but I had brothers and know all about it."

One thing was certain. He enjoyed being with Sheila Szabo. While he kept everything under control, she certainly didn't. She talked so freely about sex and emotions he wondered whether she would go to bed with him. Of course he wouldn't do it. Despite his ho-hum marriage and occasional fantasies, he had never cheated on Bonnie.

Sheila put a quarter in her meter, and they turned onto Walton where George had parked.

"Damnit, I'm about to get a ticket." He darted ahead to the SAAB where a blue-suited meter maid stood with her pen and little book. She glared at him for a second and began to write.

"Would you please take a look here. The meter went red and there's still three minutes showing."

"Sorry Mister, once it's red, that's it." She signed her

name with a flourish like she were giving an autograph.

"Let's think this through." Arrogance crept into his voice. "I paid for sixty minutes. You're giving me 57."

"Tell the judge." She walked to the front and stuck the ticket under the windshield wiper, letting the blade snap onto the glass.

He reached for his phone and focused the camera for an up-close shot, but the meter-maid walked in front of him. She shook the meter and kicked the stand, several times until the needle sprang to zero.

"Hey, you're destroying evidence." He moved around her, his arm brushing against her.

"And you're assaulting a police officer."

She walked to her three-wheeler and picked up the radio "I have an eleven-forty. Walton at Delmar." She waited, staring at George, radio cocked in her hand. He had made a terrible mistake. She would claim he had deliberately assaulted her, and from stories he had read in the paper, the courts would side with her. Furthermore she had called for help. They'd probably arrest him. No matter how fast his lawyer posted bail, he would spend time in the city jail, known to be one of the worst in the country.

"Officer." Sheila approached the scooter. A faint siren in the distance grew louder, then fainter, then louder again. "You have a tough job, especially dealing with louts like my friend here." She gestured toward George as if she were talking about a rapist.

"Are you with this man?" the meter maid asked, stepping

back. She glanced in the direction of the approaching siren. As the whine drew close, the street became deserted. People in the yards had disappeared.

"Imagine," Sheila continued, "how bad it would be if you had to work with him regularly like I do." Now came the goddamn laugh. The maid smiled, probably more at the laugh than in sympathy with Sheila. Sheila reached out, laughing louder, and put her hand on the maid's arm. They both laughed.

"Let's stuff this guy in jail," the maid said, laughing as hard as Sheila. George was pissed.

The siren rushed down Delmar toward them, making it impossible to talk. The blue-gray cruiser with the Metropolitan Police emblem on the side threatened to skid into a lamppost as it rounded onto Walton and squealed to a stop.

CHAPTER 2

"Release him to me," Sheila said. "I'll restrain him."

A patrolman, blue shirt bulging from gut and muscle, got out of the car and walked a few steps toward George. He carried his hat and as he approached, he stuffed it over his crew cut. George was afraid the man would throw him against the car like they did with black men in the Central West End. He didn't. Still looking straight at George from five feet away, he said to the meter maid, "We're answering the eleven-forty. What's the problem?"

George watched the maid. She no longer laughed. She looked down, then at Sheila and then at the patrolman who spoke again. "Is this the guy?"

"Yes." The maid hesitated, looked at Sheila. "He is, but..." She paused.

"But what, ma'am," the officer said. "If there's been an assault, we take him in." He spoke like he was in charge, as though the maid had no authority.

"I was giving this man a parking ticket and he brushed past me. It wasn't intentional."

"I don't buy that," the policeman said. "If you thought that, why the hell did you call."

They stood in silence. The maid fidgeted with her pad of tickets, pushing her pen in and out of the holder. A German Shepherd paced behind a gated-window in the rear of the cruiser. The policeman's partner had climbed out the driver's side, and as he approached, George noticed his polished belt buckle. Movement flashed behind this second officer. Two people in the window of a brick house peeked from behind half-closed drapes.

"I didn't realized at first. He was just trying to get by me."

Looks on the men's faces said they didn't believe her. The lead officer stared at George, teeth clamped over his lower lip. The air felt as still as August. George didn't realize how quiet it had become until static, and then a message crackled over the cruiser's radio. The patrolman didn't look away. Why in the hell couldn't he believe the meter maid?

"You got us out here for nothing?"

"I've handled it already." Her voice was as sharp as when she had told George to tell it to the judge.

"You better be sure."

"I'm damn sure."

"Mister, you're lucky," the officer said. "You better be careful about touching a police officer. If it were me, I'd bust your ass." The patrolman wheeled around, walked toward the car, and tossed his hat through a window. The driver gunned it and did a wide U-turn, drove back past them on Walton and swept east on Delmar.

After they were out of sight, the meter maid shook Sheila's hand. "Don't forget," she said as she hopped onto her scooter. "Keep an eye on Bozo." She shrugged toward George before driving off on her three-wheeler.

George and Sheila walked back to the clinic without a

word. Ahead he could see that the patients and staff had left the street. He imagined Sheila telling the meter-maid story with her enormous laugh. As they trudged along Delmar, he said, "I guess I ought to be thankful, but I'm going to fight this ticket. I'll need you as a witness."

"Gladly. My rate is four hundred dollars an hour, two hundred for charity cases. I've never testified in a criminal matter, though."

"A parking ticket isn't a criminal charge."

"No, but once you fight it, she'll remember the assault differently." They marched up the stairs to the clinic. "By the way I support you all the way on the ticket, but you did bump her."

"That's not an assault."

What was he doing, arguing? He sounded like a little kid on the playground trying to convince the teacher that some other kid had started the fight. All over a fifty-dollar parking ticket. He paid the damn things all the time. They walked past the clinic where the patients, who were trying to act responsibly about sex, made George feel childish.

Back in the board room they worked the printout reports for another hour. At five, Sheila said, "I have to make dinner for Debbie." They looked at their calendars and agreed to meet the same time next week.

"By the way," Sheila said at the door where she paused, her trench coat over her tennis dress, her ox-blood leather briefcase strapped to her shoulder. "Do we still need to raise money for your legal defense fund?"

She wore a smug smile.

"We'll make checks payable to PAMM," she said.

"PAM?"

"People against Meter Maids." Her laugh trailed behind as she continued down the hall.

Driving home, George imagined telling Bonnie about provocative, frolicsome Sheila. He laughed out loud about her teaming up with the meter maid. His laugh was different. A little like Sheila's. He felt light enough to float away, free to meander through the park, the long route. His to-do list was full, but for the moment he wished he could spend more time working with Sheila Szabo.

"We need to talk," Bonnie said after he kissed her cheek and she resumed stirring a pot of linguine. "Something important." Was it a dent in the station wagon, George wondered, or another fund raiser for one of her charities?

"Great" George said. "And I've got a story about my fundraising co-chair."

To the linguine Bonnie added vegetables and homemade tomato sauce riddled with sautéed garlic cloves. She worked the kitchen with the same relaxed, almost nonchalant, precision her colleagues used to admire when she was head surgical nurse at St. Ann's Hospital before Tom was born.

They ate at one end of a twenty-foot long, four-inch-thick black walnut slab that served as kitchen table, dining room table, office for Bonnie to manage the house, and work space for George.

He told Bonnie about the bomb threat and his narrow escape from arrest.

"Serves you right, treating a female cop like that," she said.

"They were an empty-headed impulse away from locking me up."

"A night in jail would teach you how women feel."

"Like a prisoner, you mean."

"Well sometimes, a willing prisoner."

"Sometimes I feel like a prisoner of my shopping-center deals that take over my life."

"Shopping centers for you," Bonnie said, "are like my stuffed dog 'Morgan' I toted everywhere as a baby. In kindergarten I had to give up Morgan, a terrible loss I replaced with accomplishments, learning a new letter of the alphabet or finishing a finger painting. Building shopping centers, kindergarten for adults, is your Morgan."

"A little more grownup," he protested.

"A little," she said.

"We could run into trouble and lose everything."

"What's the worst that can happen?" she said.

"We find dioxin when we excavate, the project stops, we spend a fortune to clean it up. We're late and over budget, lose an anchor tenant who doesn't like the delay. The bank forecloses and the foreclosure sale comes up five million short."

"Sounds pretty bad."

"The bank will insist that you sign the loan. We'd be wiped out."

"I'll give you my opinion," Bonnie said as she carried the pasta and salad bowl into the kitchen. He followed with the plates and glasses. "I have total confidence in you. I'll be glad to sign the loan. By the way I had lunch with Helen Cohen."

"Who?"

"Helen is Dean of Students at the University." George began rinsing the dishes and loading them into the dishwasher while Bonnie transferred the pasta to a bowl for the refrigerator.

"Let's clean this stuff later. I want to tell you what we discussed at lunch."

They sat back down with their wine glasses at the table where they spent so much of their time. George pictured a "pie" graph like the Family Planning Center used to show where its money went. Work took half, Bed Room a thin slice out of deference to their sex life, Social Life a little more, and except for the obligatory sliver for Other, the black-walnut-slab Dining Room Table would fill the rest.

"I ran an idea by Helen before I mention it to my women's awareness group tomorrow. I'm going to start a business."

"Oh." He intended the "oh" to sound like a question, gently asking Bonnie to go on, talk more. Instead it came out like "that's crazy."

"'Oh' what?" Bonnie said.

Bonnie's tone told him to pick his words carefully. "I thought you'd go back to nursing. I'm a little surprised at the business idea. You have the time with the kids gone. What are you thinking of?"

"A home healthcare business using nurse practitioners, physician assistants and nurses, with doctors available when needed. Helen thinks insurance companies and the government would pay to keep patients in their homes and out of hospitals. She's on the CHMO board, you know."

"CHMO? What's that?"

The City-County Health Maintenance Organization, the largest HMO in the state."

"A great idea," George said. "What about the risk of starting a business."

"Nothing like the risks of shopping centers. Helen wondered if you'd object."

"I don't object to you working." What the hell does Helen know anyway. "But what do you know about starting a business."

"I'm a competent person," she said with a mixture of impatience and exasperation. "You think it's nothing, but I've become the go-to person for fundraisers, like the hospital event this year. Round up 40 volunteers, a roomful of gifts from merchants for the silent auction, chateaus in France and the Caribbean for the live auction, a well-known chef to prepare 200 dinners for the volunteers to serve, collect all the money, and then be sure it all runs smoothly."

"You're great, but with a business there are cash flows, personnel, marketing and much more to deal with."

"I'll hire people who know finance, personnel and other areas. I've heard you talk about how to compartmentalize and limit risk."

"And hiring is the hardest of all. The best CEOs say they get it wrong half the time."

"Look, George. I know how to deal with problems. Get it wrong, make corrections."

"Honey. I just don't know. The risk scares me."

"Goddamn you."

"Settle down. I'm glad to talk about it, maybe later."

"I am settled down and we'll damn well talk about it now." She strode around the table to a sofa in the adjoining living room. He poured two coffees and walked to the couch where she was perched, not at the edge, but not comfortably at the back. Should he sit in the chair to her right or the sofa next to her? She motioned for him to put her coffee on the end table, so he set his there also and dropped into the chair.

"Please come sit next to me." Her voice fought through the hurt.

George shifted to the couch, put his arm across her shoulder and pulled her closer.

"Oh, George."

"It'll work out, honey."

"Sometimes I'm afraid I'm not worth anything."

"You're worth so much. I've always envied your ability to accomplish whatever you take on. You could probably run the Family Planning Center when Seri McQuaid retires later this year."

Shaking a finger an inch from his nose, she raised her voice and said, "You try to control everything. I don't need you to decide what I do or where I work." She stood up and walked back to the kitchen, opened the refrigerator door, reached back and flung the canister of pasta primavera. Then she stormed out the front door.

CHAPTER 3

What now? George started after her but realized it wouldn't help. Instead he paced around the house, though that wouldn't help either. He paused, considered sitting, then paced some more. What should he do? No matter what he said, she had lost it and blown up, which he hated. It pissed him off. It was he who had endured almost going to jail, had a million tasks on his to-do list. Could Bonnie handle a day like this? He was in no mood to take the blame for her problems. He hadn't done a goddamned thing. He tried to retrace the conversation but had already forgotten most of it, which always happened when they fought. All he could remember was suggesting the Family Planning Center. For trying to help he got slapped in the face.

He'd be under a lot of pressure if he and his partner built Sunset Village, their new project. He couldn't say, "fuck it," every time he ran into a problem. Run out and let the project go down the tubes. The bank would take his other shopping centers. Then their home. They'd have to rent a one-bedroom flat and live off Bonnie's business. Until she died from some disease she'd catch from one of her home healthcare patients. His imagination got as far as making her take out life insurance before he laughed at the scenario he had concocted.

He carried the cold coffee into the kitchen where he had

the urge to eat. Where does she hide the cookies? All they had were the goddamned dry ones so she wouldn't gain weight. He was surprised she didn't have a month-old sponge cake with no icing. Peanut butter and jelly left over from Tom and Robin's visit at Christmas would have to do. He went to the fridge for the grape jam and wished he hadn't. From Bonnie's heave-ho of the pasta primavera, tomato sauce was everywhere, a few drops here, globs there. A bread bag was embalmed with the stuff. Congealed noodles sat in a glob in a bowl of fresh fruit compote.

He began to move each item--the orange juice, the margarine, salad dressings, and yes, even the grape jam—from the fridge to the counter top next to the sink. He ate the garlic cloves from the pasta primavera. When the counter was full, he rinsed each object. He put the clean things on the stove next to the burners and moved more from the fridge to the counter. This logistical exercise reminded him of laying out a new shopping center. Ten minutes later, the box was empty so he cleaned it with a sponge. This would be easier if the shelves were solid. He cleaned each piece of each shelf.

Half the contents were back in the box when Bonnie walked in the back door. She had worn only a light shirt on the brisk evening. Her red nose was running and her short light brown hair was strewn around her head. "Oh, George. I'm so sorry. Please forgive me."

Was she sorry for messing up the lousy refrigerator or for how she had treated him? He decided not to ask and instead wrapped his arms around her with his check against her cold cheek. "You're forgiven," he tried to purr with mild success. "Your business will work out if that's what you want."

"It's exactly what I want. My work will be good for both of us. I'll protect us from the risks."

He remembered the great sex after their fights the first few years of marriage. The passion of anger had ignited their desire. Sex would be superb right now. George could feel the closeness it would bring. But he felt exhausted.

"Oh George, look." She pointed at the noodles bobbing in the compote. They both laughed which made him think of Sheila Szabo. His laugh sounded strange compared to Sheila's.

Instead of his office the next morning, George went to the University's Bull Market Lounge for a cappuccino, cookie and inspiration. A friendly Golden Retriever slobbered on his table as it licked some crumbs and nudged the flimsy pedestal against his leg. It found more crumbs on the floor and moved on.

George's legal pad, blank except for "Sunset Village," the name of his project, stared at him just as it had the past hour and a half. His thoughts wandered to Sheila Szabo who was going to be an enjoyable break from shopping centers.

"Vary the fucking alpha to test the differential," said one of three young men at the next table, all wearing dark suits. Business school students? Maybe they could tell him how to structure the Kreuchenmeister farm deal.

The Golden Retriever returned and found more crumbs, this time in George's lap. Before George could push her away, a woman with long stringed hair walked by and said, "Come on Rambo, we're out of here." The dog leaped to join her and in the process knocked George and his flimsy chair over backwards. His legs flew up, caught the light plastic table and sent it flying over his head.

"What the—," George caught himself before the expletive.

"Nice back-flip," said one of students. "A 10."

The woman walked over, the dog trailing, its head drooping. She looked down at the prostrate George, still tangled with the chair, coffee on his pants and shirt, and held out a hand. "I'm sorry, Mister." She pulled him up. "You okay? Rambo, shame on you. Now you be respectful." With one hand she held the dog, and with the other brushed some debris off George's shirt. "It must be springtime. Rambo's usually half dead." She picked up the table and chair.

"What's he doing here?" George said, unable to hide his irritation.

"You're right. He doesn't belong here, but I had her on a run when I got a call that a classmate needed a sub as a barista for a few hours."

George plopped the legal pad on the table and said, "Now I can get back to work," hoping to get the woman and her dog on their way.

"What you working on mister?"

"Just some work," he shrugged toward the pad.

"Sunset Village some kind of business school problem? I'm not familiar with it." The woman was tall, eye to eye with George's six feet, shoulders an inch or two wider than his. Her athletic body resembled a statue of Diana. His feeling for her shifted as he appreciated her helping out her friend as well as attending business school.

"Sunset Village will be a shopping center."

"You in the business school?" Her voice turned skeptical as though asking what the hell he was doing there. "I haven't seen you around."

"Working away from my office sometimes helps me solve problems."

"For this shopping center?"

"Trying to improve the economics before we buy the land. The owners are asking for more than I can make work."

"Sounds like the kind of case study we get in business school," she said, holding his chair for him to sit back down. Rambo lay obsequiously on the floor. "Maybe I can help."

"I'm sure you could, but I just need to think."

"Look mister, I owe you one for Rambo. Let's brainstorm."

Just what he needed, trading ideas with a business-school student. Yet he was getting nowhere on his own, plus he liked this young woman and enjoyed her enthusiasm. What did he have to lose "brainstorming" for a while?

"What's your name?" he asked after he sat down.

"Binta Brown." She pulled up a chair, its back toward the table, sat down and held out her hand.

"George Roth." They shook.

"Nice to meet you George. Now let's get to work. I've got to get home and feed Rambo. That's why she's making such a fuss. But first, a question. You going to call this shopping center Sunset Village?"

"Right."

"I hate to tell you George, but 'Sunset Village' sounds like a white folks' nursing home. No wonder the economics won't work."

George couldn't help but laugh.

"What's the matter. You don't agree?"

He didn't agree or disagree. What struck him was this neophyte telling him his head was up his posterior. She put it to him without the usual dose of ego Novocain he received from his advisors. And maybe she was right. Developers used no imagination for names. They took pride in their creativity, and then settled on "Northwood Village" for the shopping center located on the north side of town.

"What would you name it?" he asked.

"Soul City." She bit her lip and then burst out laughing. "I don't know, George. I'm only lending a hand. You'll have to name it. Hey Charles, pour us a couple of coffees," she called to the young man working behind the counter. "The name will come later. Right now we need to run some numbers, study the demographics."

"Fuck it," came from the next table. "It won't work with different variables. We'll have to ask that bastard in class tomorrow." The three young men began to stack their papers.

"Hey, you assholes" Binta called over her shoulder. "Watch your language. We got a real businessman here."

"Yeah, yeah. Screw you Binta. You do the statistics?"

"It's simple."

"Sure, sure. I bet."

"Ignore them," Binta said to George.

"They don't bother me," George said.

"Not those guys. Pay the extra amount the owners are asking for. I'm sure we can come up with ideas to make it work."

He liked Binta. Her mind worked like his partner, Harry Keys' mind had worked 15 years ago. Nimble, spontaneous, uninhibited. Every deal at some point tripped you up, sent you sprawling, made you want to call it quits. Keys had once supplied the creative energy that kept them going while George had provided the stability that kept Keys in orbit. He envied Keys' creativity and searched for his own.

"What do you think?" Binta said.

"It might work."

"Good, then I can get home and feed Rambo."

"You have a good approach. What's your background?"

"I've been around, honey. I mean George." Binta gathered up her jacket, books and a bag of muffins.

"Do you work here often?" George asked.

"Only when my friend, Sandra, has a conflict. I work for my Dad. He has different businesses. He never went to business school to learn how to be an entrepreneur, but now he sends me to this hell hole so I can take over his lumberyard. He's also the largest Black contractor in the Metro Area. Maybe he can build your shopping center."

"I'm not ready to build yet, but I'd be happy to talk with him when I am."

"Here's another idea," she said. "I know some land you can get for the right price."

"Which is why it probably won't work," George challenged.

"With the right developer it will."

"And the right contractor," he said with a smile.

"Yes sir. In fact my dad owns the land."

"How did I not guess that. By the way, I agree that you don't need business school. You're ready."

"I'm thinking a mixed-use project in the Arts District, near the museums and theaters. My dad's bought some property and keeps saying he'll do it, but never gets around to it. He's not a developer, but maybe you could do it together."

"Sounds interesting but I can only do one at a time."

"Here's my card if you want to get together. And stay away from the dead," she said as she walked toward the door, Rambo in tow.

CHAPTER 4

George changed clothes before taking his mother to lunch. He slowed at her driveway, careful not to make the same mistake as last summer when he had turned in and run over both her artificial legs. "Damn, my fault," his mother had muttered that day as she used her arms like crutches to catapult her torso and leg stumps out of an adjacent pansy bed. Her trowel hung from a rope around her neck and George's eyes were drawn to where it bounced against her chest. He gave a second look at her normally modest bust before he realized she had deposited the weeds down the front of her white cotton blouse.

Now, nine months later, he ignored the honking Chevy behind him and crawled into the driveway that was clear except for his mother's Porsche.

"I'll drive," she said. "I need an oil change and we can leave the car while we eat." With her weight on her re-built prostheses, she raised her knees, one at a time, and kicked her legs forward, a maneuver she had conquered with six months of physical therapy.

Her driving had thrilled him when he was a kid. Back when she wasn't much fun. When his father left for Viet Nam in 1970, he must have taken his mother's spunk. She reduced her life to work as an assistant librarian and anxiety at home. When George was in grade school, she wouldn't let him out to play after dinner or cross Delmar to the movies on weekends. She became the butt of his friends' jokes.

Except when she drove. Behind the wheel of the '55 Chevy his dad had souped-up, she ran yellow lights, dodged through alleys, raced men for parking spaces and accumulated enough speeding tickets for the judge to call her "Hot Rod Roth." These days the Porsche with its special hand controls was far too dangerous. Still he picked his confrontations with her carefully knowing she let go of an idea as readily as Agnes, her cat, gave up chasing birds. Besides, something inside of him, which he hated to acknowledge, enjoyed having a 77-year-old legless mother drive around town with the top down.

"Let's go," she said as she plopped her backside onto the leather upholstery. "Give me a hand with my legs."

"You ought to get an SUV," he said as he tried to fit the prostheses under the dashboard. "Much easier to get into."

"And you ought to get rid of that foreign car."

"Where'd you have in mind for lunch?" George asked as he climbed in the other side. "I need to be at the office by two."

"Harvey's Grill." She turned the ignition and eased the Porsche down the driveway.

"The greasy spoon?"

"Get a salad if you want. I'm having a cheeseburger before that so-called doctor quacks at me tomorrow about losing my vision."

His mother, who fought her diabetes with daily doses of vitamins C, B and E, something called pantothenic acid and even algae ordered from a secret lake in Oregon, couldn't resist fatty red meat. "If I go blind I'll learn to drive in Braille," she said. Meanwhile George, who worried about each new diet-health claim, would be stuck with what Harvey called a chef salad–hard chunks of white iceberg lettuce mixed with American cheese and hothouse tomatoes afloat in an oil slick.

Helen Roth, elbow jutting through her lowered window, right hand on the throttle, made a diagonal left turn out of the driveway and zipped into traffic ahead of a moving van. George gripped the door handle as though it would somehow give him control. The temperature had risen to fifty-five, brisk before the heater came to life. Approaching the back of a pickup waiting to make a left through oncoming cars, she swerved onto the apron, accelerated and ducked back onto the pavement just ahead of a sign that read, "FOR PEDESTRIANS ONLY."

"I have plenty of time," George said.

"You have less than you think."

He didn't respond. Better to let her concentrate on lane changes and pedestrians. The narrow Expressway offered challenge enough, as did the walk across eight lanes of traffic after they left the car at the service station. The aroma of cooking hamburgers, carried by the wind from the restaurant's exhaust, beckoned.

Inside, Harvey's wife ushered them to a table next to an

unhappy ficus tree. A hum of voices eddied around them forcing the waiter, dressed in khakis, a t-shirt and a waist-high apron smeared with the remains of a mustard mishap, to scream his offer of drinks.

"Jack Daniels on the rocks," Helen shouted. "Make it a double. How 'bout you, George?"

"A club soda with a lime," he said.

"Boring."

"I'd like to join you but I'm meeting Harry Keys at two."

"Not another shopping center."

"Maybe. West County."

"Isn't it about time you give up Harry Keys and shopping centers? I have no idea how you fell into this real estate stuff. You'd have thought that three years of law school would encourage you to do something noble."

A regular theme from his mother who had never cared about malls, hated shopping in them. Still his work had spit out enough for his and Bonnie's beautiful home, four years of college for Tom and Robin, even some vacations, not to mention the Porsche he had bought his mother. As to "noble," he gave his usual defense as the waiter plopped down Helen Roth's Jack Daniels and George's club soda.

"Don't forget the noble Family Planning Center. I'm working on the annual fund raising campaign."

"Snggghhhh." His mother tilted her head onto her shoulder and mimicked the sound of snoring. "Instead of volunteering, you should work fulltime for the Family Planning Center."

He wouldn't tell his mother but he had considered just that possibility. Despite his success, George had an uneasy feeling about his life. Was he capable on his own? Or merely the necessary number two for his shrewd partner, Harry Keys?

"Family planning," she continued. "A fancy name for what we used to call birth control. Find out if your date has rubbers before you hop into the back seat."

"Are we sharing intimacies now?" he said.

"Like when was the last time you had sex in the afternoon?"

"How about you?" he said, hoping to embarrass her into silence. But her voice had pierced the racket from adjacent tables. People around them were quiet, awaiting her response.

"With myself or with someone else?" she said.

He felt the smiles on the back of his neck.

"Well?"

Did she really want an answer?

"Ready yet?" The waiter paused, his left arm lined with dirty dishes.

"Good timing. Mom?"

"I'll take your large cheeseburger with five fries. No more. I'm on a strict diet. My son probably wants your no-fun salad."

The waiter flashed a smile at George. "Bring me a small cheeseburger, slaw, no fries," he said, duly bullied. And then to his mother, "A cheeseburger's not sex in the afternoon, but it's a start."

"One more idea," she said, and continued telling him how to live. She, who had hardly lived until she was his age, almost fifty, and had developed diabetes. The disease had shaken her, violently, out of a depression following his father's death in Viet Nam. Diabetes had taught her she had no time to waste. He gladly endured her suggestions until the waiter put the cheeseburgers in front of them.

"What's the doctor got in store for you tomorrow?" he asked as he set aside the grease-laden bun.

"They want to look into my arteries. I won't let them. They always tell me the same thing—I won't die if I give up living."

"It's hard to give up what you like so much."

"I can live with dying. What I can't stand is being a prisoner of the health care system."

George hated her conversations about dying. He chose to see only her strength, ignoring the frail-boned deteriorating body as though this bourbon drinking, hard driving, tongue sharpened woman could get fixed at the shop like her Porsche.

He had been on his own since the day he had graduated from high school and had worked his way through college. Still, for reasons he could never understand, life without Mom seemed uncharted, like a new journey. He had learned to mostly ignore those feelings.

"The doctors will help you," he said.

"What makes you think that?"

"That's what doctors do. They help people." George's voice had taken on a defensive tone.

"Maybe Dr. Mendoza before he died. So many of these young doctors just want to play with their expensive equipment." For a moment she sounded tired. "George, I don't want to discuss this with you, but there's one thing I need to tell you."

"What's that?"

"I've signed a living will. I don't want heroic treatment. None of those machines used on me. Promise me you won't fight this when it's time to pull the plug."

Pull the plug? He shivered. The conversation was cascading out of control. "You're doing just fine," he said.

"I couldn't be better. Still this isn't something to avoid and ignore. You might have to help me die."

"Mom, it's a long way off."

"Not that long."

He sat in the midst of the racket, isolated, nudging the last bite of the cheeseburger back and forth on his plate between the tomato and the pickle.

"George, sometimes you have to face up to things." She used her hands to pull her chair closer to the table and leaned toward him. "When it comes to helping me die, I need your solemn word."

He wanted to reach for his handkerchief to wipe the moisture from his forehead, but her eyes, locked onto his, pleaded for an answer. "I'll help you. But let's not worry about this when we don't have to."

"Tell me again. Then you can ignore it until I need you."

"You have my word."

"Thank you." They both took a deep breath. He motioned for the waiter to bring the check, and his mother stood up.

"Here take this," she said and handed him a fat envelope. "Look at it later, not now." She walked toward the door while he fumbled with his money and stuffed the envelope into his pocket.

When he followed her out, the March wind blew dirt into his eyes and for a moment the sunlight blinded him. When he looked up, she wasn't there. He looked behind and then ahead to the corner. The traffic light was still red, but there she was, doing her kick-walk back to the gas station, half-way across the eight-lane thoroughfare, like a drum majorette at the Rose Bowl. "Mom, what are you doing?" but a blaring horn from a speeding car drowned out his voice. He'd better get her before she fell. "Wait," he called. She turned to say something that flew away in the wind. The eastbound traffic in the far lanes had gone through the intersection, and Helen Roth continued against the light. By the time George reached the middle divider, she was into the sixth lane.

Right there the wind slammed into her. She teetered above the street, unable to firmly plant her legs, so instead she threw out her right arm for balance. Too late. The wind threw her to the pavement.

"Mom." He ran forward. At that moment the light turned

yellow and one more car, a cream-colored Cadillac, in his mother's lane, accelerated to beat the red light. There was no way the driver could hit the brake in time. Nor could he ease to the left without running into George. She started to rise to her knees. A long terrifying wail of the brakes flew toward her. George would never reach her. The pavement shook as rubber and metal skidded past and pivoted in a semi-circle. Rear first, the Cadillac crashed hard into a parked car in the far lane. Either the brush of metal or blast of wind had thrown his mother back onto the pavement.

CHAPTER 5

"Mom. Mom, are you okay?" George knelt beside her.

"These legs aren't worth a damn." She struggled to one knee.

"Wait for an ambulance." He tried to lower her gently onto the pavement.

"Ambulance, my..." Her voice trailed off as she shrugged his hand away and tried to get back on her feet. Unable to set the prostheses, she fell to her hands and knees and crawled toward the Cadillac. First an arm, followed by the stump and plastic leg from the opposite side. Then the other arm and other leg. Her rigid legs and supporting arms gave the appearance of a child's toy robot.

What am I doing sitting here watching? His mother needed help and God knows the condition of the driver. The car the driver had hit was folded in the center like an empty beer can. George looked toward the curb to see if anyone he knew was watching him sit on his butt. Thankfully, no one, but shame over his vanity replaced his relief.

His mother was no more than ten feet from the Cadillac when the driver's door opened with a screech of metal against metal. The left side had partially collapsed forcing the driver to squeeze through a narrow opening, first a head and shoulder, followed by a leg. A long exhale freed his chest and stomach. In his gray business suit, stained with blood or grease from the door, the man stalked around the Cadillac. Fist shaking and mouth churning, he advanced on Helen Roth. Hair stuck out from the top of his round head in four or five directions. He was probably in shock, so agitated that George was afraid he might kick her.

"Lady, you have no business…"

"Sir, are you okay? I'm so sorry." His mother reached toward him.

He stopped short and deflated in front of her, like a punctured balloon. With her legs dragging behind her body, she had become an absurd target of his rage. By the time George reached her, the man had retreated and sat on the curb.

Someone must have called the police. An officer arrived, as did an ambulance. The policeman questioned the driver, George and other witnesses, while a medic examined George's mother and wrapped a blood-pressure cuff around her arm.

"I'm fine," she kept saying. "Look after the man," whom the medic ignored as he checked her vital signs.

"You seem okay." He examined her pupils and gently rotated each limb.

"Looking at that car," the policeman said to the medic, "it's amazing that guy seems to have only a few abrasions. "Why don't you take a look at him."

And to George, "You ought to get her home."

George picked his mother up—she weighed only

ninety-five pounds with the prostheses—and carried her to the car. She shook in his arms. Or was it he who shook?

"What a clumsy clod I am," she sighed.

"You're doing fine." The lecture could come later. Before she could object he set her in the passenger seat, paid for the lube job and ducked behind the wheel. "I'm taking you to the doctor's."

"Absolutely not. You have your meeting with Keys."

"You come first."

"I can't just walk into the doctor's without an appointment. They'll send me to the emergency room."

"Tell you what. I'd like to calm down before my meeting. I'll take you home so we can both get settled." If she were okay, he'd see Keys. If not, the business could wait. Meanwhile he could use some time to let his adrenalin settle.

Two hours later, George walked into the Keys/Roth suite. Down the hall, framed by the door to his office, stood Harry Keys, dressed in boxer shorts and no shirt, holding barbells chest-high in the middle of a squat, his face a red balloon about to burst. The sight and faint odor reminded George of the wrestling room back in the high school gym. Keys dropped the weights to the mat with a thud that shook the suite.

"It's good we're the landlord here," George called out as

he poured a coffee in the small room they used as a kitchen. He would never have guessed Keys would take himself so seriously. At their first office they used to clown around with a basketball in the parking lot, play some horse after lunch. Sometimes they received phone calls for a plumber who had a similar number. One evening Keys answered a call about eight-thirty as they were putting together a proposal, and said, "Yes sir, we'll be right over." George tried to talk him out of it, but in the end they bought a wrench and poked around some family's basement for an hour while an anxious man in a bathrobe told his two sleepy-eyed kids not to "bother the nice men." They actually repaired the pipe.

George disposed of some emails and considered his life as a real estate developer. Success had earned them more money and less pleasure. The pleasure of going to work had evolved into a job. He used to feel sorry for friends who dreaded Mondays and called Wednesdays the hump. Not that he hated what he did. Only that pressure to repeat each success and prove his worth had replaced the fun and adventure.

He walked down the hall to Keys' office and stepped over the bar bells. "Hey Sport, have a seat," Keys said. He sat shirtless at his desk, a towel around his neck. Even though he had constructed his space without windows that might interrupt his concentration, double strength bulbs made the room as bright as a police lineup. His sweat caught the light.

"What's up, Champ?" Keys said. At one time those words signaled he was ready for a break, for some fun, perhaps a story. Now his sparkle was hollow, except when wooing important outsiders.

"You get those hicks to come down half a million?" Keys asked.

"They won't budge," George said, referring to the Kruechenmeisters, owners of the only remaining West County farm large enough for a major shopping center. The Kruechenmeisters didn't like Keys, so that George had taken over the negotiations. George enjoyed dealing with Hazel and Herman Kruechenmeister, hardly country bumpkins but rather a nice couple who soon would enjoy retirement as millionaires.

"No rush," Keys said. He ran the towel over his face. "He's an old man who'll beg us to take his property when the spring rains threaten his planting season."

"You ever heard of Emanuel Brown?" George asked.

"A Black guy, involved in city politics?"

"Probably the same. I met his daughter while I was working at the business school coffee shop. A bright young woman. Said her father had some property to sell in the Arts District."

"And you want to buy it," Keys said. "Do a rehab and lose all your savings."

"The District's perfect for a mixed-use development. They need housing, people are moving their offices to the city. There are plenty of retail opportunities."

"A couple of guys trying to gentrify poor people's neighborhoods. Our pictures will be on the front page." Keys referred to what had become a major complaint as the middle class had moved back to the parts of the city it had abandoned 50 years ago for the suburbs.

"We could get some grants for affordable housing and create a diverse community. Raise money by selling the rehab tax credits." Some energy worked its way into George's thoughts. Exciting to do something new rather than "a white person's nursing home." He smiled recalling Binta's words. Not only new, but even worthwhile, affordable housing, people living near where they worked, using less gasoline, the Arts District even more attractive for visitors.

The telephone rang. "Grab it, Dolores," Keys shouted. "Remember I got the tanning salon at four-thirty."

The ringing stopped but Dolores, plump and smiling as usual, appeared at the door. "It's Mr. Smith from the bank. About the expansion loan."

Keys grimaced. "We have to take this," he said as he flipped on the speaker phone.

"Spencer, I'm here with George Roth."

"Hi Spencer," George said. He didn't like the prissy Spencer Elliot Smith, who came to life when he foreclosed a mortgage.

"Good afternoon, George."

"Spence baby, I hear you landed the Brookings business." Keys picked up a tight-gripped hand exerciser and began squeezing. "You guys are out of your minds. You'll be the biggest bank in town."

"We hold our own," Smith said with obvious pride.

"You bet you do," Keys' melodic voice purred.

"Your loan looks good for the Mid County Mall expansion," Smith said. "Fifteen years, five percent..." While Smith droned on, George's mind wandered. George had arranged the partners' first loan at Mid County Mall, and had taught Keys the basics of borrowing money. In those days, Keys cheered him up after George's fights with Bonnie, before marriage counseling evened out but flattened their relationship. Keys, a bachelor, had amused George with descriptions of romances with women twenty years older and ten years younger. The former Miss Missouri only had sex standing up so she wouldn't disturb her hair. The six-two, all legs basketball star from Southern Illinois University convinced the six-five Keys to add a small gym to his house so they could shoot baskets naked.

As partners, George and Keys hadn't conquered the world, but over the last twenty years they had built their office building plus four shopping centers, had had some fun, at least at first, and had become financially secure, at least on paper. George had money in the bank and a nice income. Hard to know what the shopping centers were worth as the country was still recovering from a recession, and online sales continued to take away shopping center business.

"Participation?" Keys asked with a tone of disbelief that

jolted George back to the speaker phone. "You want ten percent of the expansion?"

"Shopping centers are not our priority right now," Smith said. "We think they're risky. If a participation is a problem, you might want to try one of the other banks."

"Not a problem. Take a twenty percent participation and slice a half percent off the interest rate."

Silence followed as undoubtedly Smith was calculating the effect of this suggestion. Keys switched the exerciser to his left hand.

"I'll think about it," Smith said. "Meanwhile I'll send you these terms."

"We appreciate it, Spence," Keys said. "How about that West County development I mentioned, that farm we're trying to buy?"

"The county is overbuilt. If you sign an anchor tenant, we'll talk about it."

"Spencer, thanks for calling." Keys smiled as he clicked off the speaker. "I have him scratching his head over why I'd offer twenty percent. Before we're done I'll get rid of this participation in exchange for another half a point." The smile on Keys' face spread to delight before he added, "No one screws up the thinking of a guy across the table in a negotiation like I can."

George gathered his papers and was almost out the door when Keys said, "One more thing before I have to get out of here. I had a call the other day from a man I haven't seen in years. He says we're in for trouble because you're into that abortion thing. With the 'evil Family Planning Center,' the guy says."

"I've been on the Board of Directors for 15 years. Hasn't been a problem."

"And maybe isn't now. But we need to keep an eye on it. Why not give it up and volunteer more with Legal Assistance." George had never practiced law other than as a volunteer with the Legal Assistance organization which had him do intakes in the city once a month at a foodbank run by the Archdiocese.

CHAPTER 6

George arranged to meet Binta Brown on Saturday to drive the Arts District. Probably no project there, but he'd enjoy a morning with Binta.

On his way he stopped to check in on his mother's, slowly entering the driveway. The front of her house with the flower bed where the large sycamore used to be home base for hide-n-seek, looked smaller than when he was a kid. The makeup of the neighborhood had changed dramatically. Only three white families now lived on the block.

Helen Roth refused to move. "I love my house," she always said. "Besides, people here are nice to me. More fun since Blacks moved in." This was the same woman who forbade George from going to the integrated pool in the seventies.

He found her tossing grass seed in back. "It never grows," she said, "which doesn't keep me from trying."

"Looks like you're feeling ok after that fall."

"A few aches and pains, but I didn't need a fall to have those."

"I brought you a cappuccino. How about a break?"

"After I finish. You can roll that fertilizer thing."

The coffee aroma mixed with the fresh air in the yard until the fertilizer "aroma" took over. Eventually they sat at the top of the porch steps, a few feet behind where home plate had been when he was growing up.

"You ready for your debate?" she said in a voice that suggested she didn't think he was.

"I will be."

"This is your chance to stomp 'em."

"People should listen to each other, not wage war," he said. Since the bomb scare he had regained his hope for a reasoned debate.

"Don't wimp around, George." She sounded like his high school football coach.

"I'll talk about tolerance. They're entitled to their views."

"Mental masturbation." She gave her crotch a quick rub. "Put some heat into it," which made him imagine Sheila Szabo explaining heat and sex to her teenage daughter.

"We need less emotion about abortion," he said.

"Baloney. We need a woman to handle this debate. You namby, pamby this thing, and that Cordry dame'll walk all over you." He wished he had told her about Binta Brown rather than discuss the debate. He stood up and she did also using first the steps and then George's arm for leverage. "They repeal Roe v. Wade…" she said, "there'll be a holy war. Here, toss my cup in the trash on your way out."

"That's my daddy's property." Binta gestured toward a grey brick building.

"The drug store's been there since I was a kid," George said. "My dad used to take the streetcar down here and transfer to get to the ballpark."

"That drug store's been there since the Lewis and Clark Expedition," Binta said. "Which by the way was the beginning of white colonization of Native American land west of the Mississippi."

"We were taught they were heroes."

"We look at our country's history differently than you."

"Both have validity. Are the top floors occupied?"

"No and yes."

"No and yes?"

"No. The history the state forced you and me to read doesn't have validity, but we can talk about that another day. Yes. We have tenants up above."

George wanted to say more, ask Binta about the harsh treatment her ancestors had received, glossed over by so many in the country. How did unequal treatment affect her and her family? "I can't imagine your reality."

"Whatever. We're here for business, not history or culture. Someday we'll talk about it."

"I'd like that."

Any project in this area would require the Browns' cooperation plus ample racial sensitivity operating in the half-Black city. He had some fundamental business questions before he got there.

"Any rehab would make your tenants homeless. I wouldn't do that even if the City let me."

"My daddy has plenty of apartments folk can move to. Some temporary, some permanent."

They continued south on Grand Avenue and made a U-turn through a fast-food parking lot just past the Interstate. George drove slowly as Binta pointed out development opportunities.

"You're a young guy, George. This'll keep you busy the rest of your life so you won't need Sunset Village."

"I'd need two lifetimes for a project here."

They drove past the university and George wondered how much of the land it owned for expansion. Binta didn't know but thought the university, with its huge investment in the area, would cooperate or at least approve a development. "Their money and political influence could be a big help."

George imagined meeting with the university president, the mayor, the Archbishop, business leaders, and community leaders. This project would have more challenges than he previously had faced. Would Keys even participate? George would take on roles he hadn't significantly played in the past, a grandiose fantasy, which he enjoyed. He had no experience with community leaders in a Black community. He'd need help.

They parked to get a cup of coffee.

"The evil empire," Binta said.

"Starbuck's? Their ingenuity with products and marketing makes them successful, but that doesn't qualify them for the evil empire."

"You need some Black blood to appreciate the underdog."

"Black people should be prominent in a project here. Why doesn't your father do it?"

"He'd love to do the construction, but he's not a real estate developer."

"I'd like to meet him."

"Maybe, maybe not."

"Maybe not what?" George said as he dipped into the whipped cream that had sunk to the bottom of his cup.

"He's not as lovable as I am."

"No one's as lovable as you, Binta. Would I survive?"

"I'd enjoy finding out. This isn't West County."

West County wasn't that simple. George and Keys had dealt with government officials in several communities, neighbors who loved developments as long as they weren't too near their million-dollar homes, environmentalists suing to preserve trees. One community gave them the go-ahead only when they included an atrium with a tree growing through the shopping center roof. He was intrigued to meet Emanuel Brown.

CHAPTER 7

"How're you doing with the farmers, "Keys asked as he walked into George's office, dressed in his sweats, stirring a protein supplement.

"Still a half million apart."

"Need help?"

"You could entertain them, take them to a ballgame in your luxury box. I took them to dinner last night. The missus throws down the bourbon. I have a bad hangover." The fluorescent lights nailed him to his chair. Meeting with Sheila Szabo after lunch would be a lot more enjoyable without this headache.

"I'll fly them to Florida. Find a winter home to buy with the money we'll give them. They won't have to pay state income tax in future years." Keys walked down the hall and returned with a pot of coffee.

"Do you remember when I mentioned Binta Brown?" George said.

"You met her at the business school."

"I drove the Arts District with her. Saw her father's property on Grand."

"She good looking?

"Decide for yourself when we do a deal with her father."

"You're always the dreamer. Meanwhile see if the Kreuchenmeisters would like a Florida vacation. Soon the weather's going to improve and the old man will have to work the fields. Let's get him down there before the hurricane season."

George called Hazel Kreuchenmeister and asked to meet the next day, told her he wanted to make them rich.

On the way to the Family Planning Center, George thought about sex with Sheila, comfortable that the seduction would take place only in his mind. He had passed up opportunities for affairs in the past. Last year, a summer intern, the daughter of one of their bankers, had brushed against him several times as they stood over some spread sheets at his desk. That night over a Scotch with Keys at the Watering Hole, George mentioned her. Keys, who screwed every female in their office except his own secretary, with whom he "had too important a relationship," said, "That's fantastic. I was going to hit on her, but you go ahead."

"Not me."

"On the plus side, she's great looking, nice body. At worst I'd piss off a banker but bankers are a dime a dozen."

"You sound like you're buying a piece of land. Weighing the pros and cons."

"A good way to look at it. Avoid a bad buy."

The potential reality of an affair was too complex for George. Secret meetings, cryptic phone conversations around Bonnie, eventually tears and threats. Bonnie would find out and life would be a mess. Wild sex and an uninvolved relationship might be great, but it never remained that way in his fantasies. So he passed up potential opportunities, a little ashamed his reason wasn't more righteous than adultery was too complicated.

Flirting with sassy Sheila felt safe and secure.

"Guess the first thing I notice when I see you," Sheila said as he sat down at the table. A smile skipped across her face, reminding him of a twelve-year-old's mischief as the teacher walked out of the room.

"My abundant wisdom?"

"Nope."

"My expanded pecks from swimming all winter?"

"Of course your pecks, but that's not what I noticed today."

A siren passing on Delmar worked its way through two sets of walls and faintly into the windowless board room. George ignored the sound and tried to figure out what Sheila had observed.

"Better tell me."

"The hairs in your nose."

She startled more than embarrassed him. Without thinking, he said, "What I notice about you, Sheila, is your great bod." Where the hell had that come from, he wondered.

She roared, and for a brief moment cupped her hands under her boobs and said, "These? You noticed these?" She reached out, touched his hand and said, "Don't blush. I'm pleased you noticed."

"Forgive me." Her hand felt good but he drew back.

"You're forgiven. Let's get to work." She wiped the smile off her face. But then, seemingly against her will, laughed again.

He laughed, right on top of her laugh, and she wasn't even being funny.

Hiding a snicker, she shoved him a printout and the telephone, picked up another list and walked across the room to another phone. They called last year's solicitors, asked if they would work again and asked for information about donors. One donor had stopped giving because the Family Planning Center did so many abortions, while another had stopped because they provided too little abortion support. Why couldn't people be rational about abortion?

As he was about to make another call, Sheila said "We need a theme for the campaign."

"How about 'just say no.' It appeals to conservative donors with money."

"George, I'm for that 'no' stuff too. Trouble is, good intentions don't always--"

A loud bang like a blowout on a speeding car cut her short. The board room shook as if there were an earthquake. George and Sheila stared at each other. They leaped up, scrambled to the door and down the hall toward the stairway. Before they reached the clinic, the door to the waiting room flew open. People flooded out and knocked them back against the wall. "Goddamn it," Sheila muttered as she fell and landed on her side. George reached to help her, but didn't have room as the crowd ran by. Sheila strained for George's hand, her taut face and terrified eyes screaming for help. Now the people, having run the wrong way, rushed past in the other direction, knocking him onto Sheila. Neither had room to maneuver so they lay tangled together. A cloud of black smoke unfolded down the corridor along with a rank odor. Screams filled the hallway, which was too small to absorb the noise. A teenager with terror on her face fell next to them, and others tripped over her.

"Everyone stay calm," said Seri McQuade in a loud voice that somehow didn't sound like a shout. "Walk, don't run, that way, away from my voice. Be extra careful on the stairs." People began to move.

George got to his feet and helped Sheila and others. They waited with Seri for the corridor to empty. The crowd was quiet.

"Are you okay?" George asked Sheila.

"My shoulder hurts. I'll be okay once we get out of here."

As the last patients walked down the stairs, he heard a sound, maybe a voice, maybe a moan. From the waiting room. Quickly he stepped in, but bounced back from the smoke, his eyes watering. The smoke and odor, burning rubber, made it difficult to think. A woman was crying. "Where are you?" George said. The sounds came from the floor to his left. On hands and knees, he crawled until he bumped into a table. Amidst the smoke he saw the woman. She was on her belly beneath the table, arms wrapped around two little boys. They couldn't be much more than a year.

"This way," George tugged at her elbow. "We gotta get out of here." The woman jerked away, sobbing.

On his knees, George moved the table and then tried to lift the woman. The two toddlers, separated from their mother, began to wail. They were twins. One shrieked and the other plugged his ears with his palms.

"My baby, my baby," the woman said.

"I'll help them, but we have to get down to the street," George tried to coax her. Flames could explode any second.

"No, my baby."

Then he saw the tiny infant underneath the woman, maybe a month old. The baby was so small George was afraid the woman had smothered it. He offered to help but the woman refused to get off.

With one hand George lifted her and with the other the infant. He began to drag the woman toward the door. "Crawl," he commanded the twins who followed. On the stairs, Seri took the baby, a girl, while Sheila and George carried the twins and led the woman.

"My babies," she said over and over.

Outside two fire engines and an ambulance had arrived. Fire fighters burst past George up the stairs. Patients and staff stood on the sidewalk, staring at each other. Or at the building. Most seemed not to notice the passersby who asked what had happened. George shook. He felt numb. Sheila stood in silence, as though in a trance, rubbing and then rotating her arm. She stretched the neck of her double knit sweater over her shoulder and George saw a crimson blotch. A teenage girl babbled to no one in particular, "Hey man, like hey man, it was loud." Then her tears flowed as though her words had made her realize what she had been through. Blood ran down the forehead of another teen, the one who had fallen upstairs; a woman patted the gash with a handkerchief. As smoke seeped out second-story windows, traffic backed up on Delmar in both directions.

George led the woman he had helped, who had retrieved her baby from Seri, up the block away from the crowd. Sheila carried the twins. He sat the woman on a sofa outside the antique shop, and Sheila set a twin on each side of her. Observing the woman for the first time, George realized she was only a girl. She looked like Robin when she was in tenth grade.

George knelt next to her and said, "You'll be okay now."

She responded with a stream of tears, and when she tried to talk, some coughs. Finally, between sobs, she said, "My caseworker sent me..." She couldn't continue. Convulsive cries stuffed her words. Sheila sat on the edge of the couch and held her for what seemed a long time. "I want to stop having babies and get a job or go back to school. But I'm not coming here again. I'm not even going up for my coat." She shivered.

"Here, put this on." George took off his sweater and

helped her pull it over her shoulders. It was large enough to cover the twins at her sides and soon they were giggling and playing "peek-a-boo" out the neck. George laughed for a moment, but the girl's words and despair fueled his anger. He wanted to take a swing at whoever was responsible for shattering the girl's hopes.

He left Sheila with the girl and kids and strode up the street. In front of the clinic, patients were saying the bomb had been in the waiting room. George mixed with the people and asked questions to see if everyone had gotten out.

A few minutes later a fireman stepped out the door carrying a smoking pot. The other firemen appeared and mulled around. One approached Seri, whom apparently he knew. "Strips of burning rubber. We got it all, but you'll have smoke damage." He held out a piece of paper to the policeman in charge, a message made from newspaper cutouts. "This is a warning to the baby killers," the officer read.

"One of these days," the fireman said, "they're going to kill someone. I'm surprised they didn't this time."

When it was safe, patients and staff climbed the stairway for their belongings. George returned to the antique shop.

"It's over now," he said to the girl on the couch.

"They would have run right over my baby if I hadn't put her under a table," the girl said. "I'm not going back."

"I'm sure it's safe," George said. "How about if I carry the boys?"

He helped her up, dropping the giggling twins out the sides of his sweater, and walked with them up the street toward the clinic. At the stairs the mother balked. "I won't go in."

"This has been a terrifying experience," Sheila said.

"You know it, Ma'am."

"I feel afraid too."

"Going up there's not for me."

"It's safe now, but I understand if you don't want to go," Sheila said.

The girl shook her head, so Sheila went for her coat and called a cab. The girl had no car and her mother, with whom she lived, was at work. Sheila returned with a dozen condoms and found George writing down the girl's name and address. "Oh look, Sheila brought some rubbers," he said.

"Boys won't use them," she said as she cried. The bitter edge on her words magnified her sense of being powerless, a reaction George felt in his gut.

"We have IUDs and female condoms," Sheila said. "Tell me your phone number and we'll follow up to get you fitted."

She hesitated but Sheila coaxed it out of her.

When the cab came, George gave her forty dollars and helped the family into the back seat. Sheila and he watched in silence as they drove off. Two hours before, he couldn't have comprehended someone so young with three children. In her life, he would have felt defeated. She must have resilience to have gotten her toddlers this far. Maybe they had a chance. But chances wouldn't matter if she got no help.

CHAPTER 8

"I'm a wreck," Sheila said. "Take me for a drink."

She clutched his arm as they walked toward the Central West End. A knot in his stomach had replaced his rage. The odor of burning smoke had lodged in his nose, reminding him how sometimes he still smelled tear gas from ROTC gas-mask training 30 years ago.

"You were wonderful," Sheila said. "Helping that girl and her kids."

He had merely reacted, yet Sheila's acknowledgment made him feel good about how, without thinking, he had retrieved the family.

They walked without talking for a block. After crossing Delmar, Sheila said, "Our house burned to the ground when I was a kid. That smoke and that poor girl brought it all back." She tightened the grip on his arm.

"You were a big help." George tried to reassure her.

They passed a white-tablecloth restaurant, and walked into Winston's, another joint that claimed to be a stopping-off point for the Lewis and Clark Expedition. George used to take Bonnie to Winston's after her nursing shifts, and these days Bonnie complained that George worked so hard they couldn't get there more often. A barrel of peanuts, full for the approaching happy hour, sat by the door and shells crunched beneath their shoes on the hardwood floor. They took the last empty booth, next to the foul line for the dart board.

Sheila rested her elbows on the table and her head in her hands. "How old were you when your house burned down?" he asked.

"Twelve," she sighed. After a moment, she raised her head and her words overflowed. "My Dad had split the year before. My Mom and I had to get the four younger kids out of the fire. Bring me a Stinger," she said to the passing waiter. George ordered a Black Label without water or ice. Sheila seemed to be recalling the experience as she sat quietly.

"Mom never recovered after Dad left. I wasn't much support because I blamed her for his leaving. Now I think he took off because he couldn't face having five children." The waiter dropped off the drinks and Sheila gulped down half the Stinger. "As it turned out, Mom also couldn't handle the kids. I spent a lot of time taking care of my brothers and sister."

The Scotch burned on the way to George's stomach. Gripped by Sheila's emotional portrayal of her dramatic childhood, he took her hands in both of his and said, "So tough to grow up like that."

"Which is why I'm involved with the Family Planning Center. Parents should want their children."

"You work as well."

"I'm a health care consultant."

"You mean a doctor?"

"No, no." There went the laugh again, rolling out toward

him and then she pulled it back. "I consult about business matters with doctors, HMO's, insurance companies and the like."

The bar was filling up with people and their voices, forcing George to lean forward. "What kinds of things do you consult about?"

"Any and every. Patient flow, clinic-physician relations, long-range planning, technology needs. I'm a generalist. I know next to nothing about almost everything."

Like his mother, Sheila had confidence and certainty about her life. No wonder she could raise a daughter, run a business, promote the Family Planning Center, even fit in her tennis game. She raised a family before she was even a teenager. Maybe the challenge had launched her life.

"How about you?" Sheila said. "What got you involved with women's rights?"

He usually answered this question with a speech about government imposing one group's morality onto others. Yet for Sheila, without really thinking why, he told about Miss Riley, his first-grade teacher. Miss Riley had disappeared right before Thanksgiving. All fall she had bestowed her warmth on George as though aware that his father was in Viet Nam and that his mother wasn't available for him. He still recalled how she couldn't control her enthusiasm when she read out loud, taking on the voices and dialects of each character, quacking and oinking. Miss Riley never came back. A substitute took over and no one told them why. Until his mother, ten years later, let drop, acting as if he had known all along, that Miss Riley had died having an illegal abortion.

"Makes me furious," Sheila said. "Miss Riley meant so much to you."

The warmth from Sheila's understanding magnified his memory of the loss.

After a few moments he drew his hands away, took a drink of Scotch, and said, "Is Debbie your only child?"

"Yes, and planned."

"Do you think about having more?"

"I'm divorced and have my hands full with Debbie plus work. Not likely now."

Soon it would be dark and maybe unsafe to walk back to their cars, but Sheila was into a second Stinger as well as her story. Another Scotch eased his anxiety, made it easier to listen. "I grew up wild," Sheila said. "A full time job in college didn't keep me from hitting every party." She even found time to be the den mother for a YWCA youth group. "Like everyone else back then, I fought, I played, I made love and I assumed mine was the only way. You're such a good listener. Now I want to hear about your youthful adventures."

He was shocked when he looked at his watch. "It's almost seven-thirty. I need to call home."

Outside waiting for Bonnie to answer, he was aware of how easy it was to talk with Sheila, how understanding, open and spontaneous she was. Bonnie's voicemail answered, and he left a message he wouldn't be late.

Back at the table Sheila said, "You're in so much trouble already, I got you another drink."

"Bonnie must be at a meeting so I might as well."

They ordered hamburgers, his second in a week, twice his yearly allotment. He felt a glow from the Scotch. Sheila, who said she hardly ever drank, switched to Courvoisier, and shared the snifter with George. The evening reminded him of times when he was single and was instantly compatible with a date, every detail from their lives fresh. He told Sheila about Harry Keys.

"A challenging relationship for you," she said and for a brief moment she laid her hand on his again. The touch was reassuring, different from when she had hung onto his hand when they first arrived at Winston's.

"At times enjoyable and profitable." He resisted telling her about conflict with Bonnie over starting a business.

At quarter to ten they talked about when they would meet again. She was leaving for spring vacation with Debbie on Monday so they agreed on the end of the month. He walked her to her car, glowing with infatuation he both hoped and feared would be gone with tomorrow's reality. Euclid was well lit but deserted. Teenagers, crazed with drugs, committed armed robberies on Euclid. He took Sheila's arm and walked faster. She seemed to understand.

At the car Sheila turned and said goodnight. Without thinking George put his arms around her shoulders and kissed her. For a moment her mouth opened and her tongue pushed back. Then she said, "Sometimes life needs mouth-to-mouth resuscitation." Before he could answer, she was in the car, driving away.

George looked after the tail lights until they merged with the traffic on Delmar. He wanted to reach out and pull her back, but he sensed the danger that came with his excitement. While Bonnie didn't leave him short of breath, she was predictable and safe. With the thought about safety, he walked to his car.

At home all lights were out. He tiptoed to the bedroom, but Bonnie wasn't there. A message on his phone said she was meeting some nurse practitioners about her business. Though he wondered how her meeting could go this late, the stress and the booze had taken over, so he stripped and fell into bed. About midnight he woke and Bonnie still wasn't home. He began to worry about her being out late and driving home alone. Images, semi-conscious dreams of Bonnie being robbed or in an accident, or could she be having an affair, played through his mind. When he slept, he dreamt that Sheila, on a broom stick, was chasing him. She looked beautiful, not like a witch. Then she was putting on her tennis dress, covering her breasts just before they came into view. She was playing a match against Bonnie, who has his mother's face from forty years ago, rigid and austere, a scary face. He sat up and saw Bonnie asleep beside him.

CHAPTER 9

The coffee was dripping by the time George got out of bed. Without doubt, Bonnie's business was an energy booster even if it came to nothing.

"Late last night," George said.

"Any problem with that?"

"I was a little worried around midnight." He dodged around her to the cereal in the cupboard. After 25 years of marriage, they had the breakfast ballet down pat.

"I've never learned to stop worrying when you have night meetings," she said.

"How did it go?" He poured the milk, added a banana and some sugar, and ate while they talked at the black walnut table.

"A splendid night. I had dinner with 3 of my cronies from hospital days. They love their work but hate their jobs in today's medical climate."

"Understandable. Half of my annual physical involved the doctor dictating notes to her nurse to put into the computer, which the doctor didn't know how to do."

"My friends say they'd have no trouble toting a computer to home visits."

"Sounds like you're off to a good start."

"They want to join me, even willing to start at less pay."

George liked hearing about Bonnie's business regardless

of how well it did. Her being busy made him less responsible for her happiness. Maybe her business would absorb her life as much as his business absorbed his. Bonnie in meetings, even after midnight, would provide more flexibility for his schedule.

Over a second cup of coffee he told her about the bomb and a little about Sheila's background. "She might have ideas about your business," he said.

"I'd like to meet her. By the way, I noticed this in the bedroom. I went by to check on your mother yesterday and she asked if you had mentioned it." She handed George an envelope that he recognized as the one his mother had handed him at their lunch.

"From my mother who's after me to pull the plug on her life if she gets sick. Let's take a look." Along with the Advanced Health Care Directive, was a note.

"My dear George, Who works too hard and doesn't have enough time for Bonnie. So please do an old woman a favor. Accept the enclosed tickets to Paris and a prepaid week at the Ritz. You both deserve it. If you must, visit a French shopping center. Love, Mom"

Bonnie said, "Wow. This would be great before you start your next deal and I get too involved in my business."

"Perfect." He held her close, happy the fight the other night was behind them. The Ritz reservation for the middle of May would motivate him to accomplish enough to deserve a vacation. He didn't want to wait until retirement, when they'd be another pair of senior citizens thankful for a bus tour through the Alps.

"I've got to get going," he said. "Got an appointment with the farmers whose land we need to buy."

"We're having dinner with the Wennings," Bonnie said. "I'll run the dishwasher and you can empty it when you get home." George realized that Bonnie going back to work would toss more of the domestic chores into his lap, where many had been before she gave up her job to raise the children. He recalled an ad for a carpet-sweeping robot whose time had come.

CHAPTER 10

The Kruechenmeisters' black Lab growled and sprang across the yard toward George who had parked next to a statue of the Virgin Mary propped up in a bathtub. The old tub with three-toed feet would fetch a good price at the antique shop down the block from the Family Planning Center. The dog's growl rolled into a snarl and then an accusatory bark as she crossed the yard, despite a limp, too fast for George to retreat to the car.

"Chipper, stop that," called Hazel Kruechenmeister as she followed her voice out the back door of the farmhouse. "You know Mr. Roth." A stroke had left Chipper with the limp. The Kruechenmeisters used to keep her behind a fence so she wouldn't chase squirrels and have another stroke, but being a prisoner made her so unhappy, they let her run loose. If Chipper could write an Advanced Health Care Directive, running loose would be her number one direction.

"We're still friends," George said with more hope than confidence. Chipper sniffed his shoes and then his legs up to his crotch. George leaned down and ran both hands through the mutt's shoulders until she raised up and gave him a thorough face lick.

"George, it's so good to see you," Hazel Kruechenmeister said, drawing out the "good" and making it sound like he was special. She gave him a hug against her ample bosom.

He could never quite identify her smell, perhaps a mixture of a pie she'd been cooking with a mustiness from her shirtwaist dress. "Please come in." She took him by the arm and led him through the kitchen.

Mixed-use in the Arts District had romance, but Sunset Village was reality. His financial projections showed a modest return if they paid no more than two million seven hundred thousand for the land. The Kruechenmeisters had refused to budge below three million. Keys was stuck at two million five.

"The coffee's fresh," Hazel said. "I'll cut you a piece of apple pie I made for Mr. Kruechenmeister for dinner." While apple-pie-in-the-morning challenged George's concern for his waistline, the smell of warm cinnamon convinced him it would be rude to turn down his host.

She always sat him at the dining room table across from the mirror. The reflection showed a painting of Jesus on the wall behind him, three feet high, a foot and a half wide.

Hazel set down the coffee and pie and plopped into her chair. She was short from the waist up so that her bosom almost rested on the table. "George, I hope you brought your check book so I can get Mr. Kruechenmeister off that tractor and down to Florida six months a year."

"I brought it, but we have to talk price."

"Talk all you want, but he'll just turn you down like he's turned down developers for years. Another excuse to keep the farm."

"The rents I can charge for the stores won't support the

price he wants. I'll try to explain this to him. If we can't make a deal, maybe he'll at least let me drive the tractor." He tried to sound unconcerned.

Her smile showed her front-tooth's gold crown. "Now George you know he won't let anyone onto his tractor. You'll have a harder time buying his equipment than his land. There goes that dog again. Mr. K will be along shortly. Here, let me warm your coffee."

Hazel left her own half-full cup next to an open catalog. Even though the Kruechenmeisters lived less than 5 miles from Westview, one of those tube-like malls, grafted to four department stores, Sears, Penney, Dillards and Macy's, Hazel still did most of her shopping from the catalog. Twice a year, for Christmas and then for their winter trip to Florida, she dressed up Mr. Kruechenmeister and drove him to Westview. They spent a day and bought a few hundred dollars of clothes, plus whatever presents they needed for six children and 19 grandchildren. Otherwise if they left the farm, they drove west, across the Missouri River to a cafe where they would eat a plate dinner for $8.40 at the Corner Cafe. They would wander Main Street and visit their banker who paid a percent-and-a-half less on CD's than banks in the city but knew the Kruechenmeisters' children and grandchildren.

Chipper's bark grew louder, and then the front door swung open. Herman Kruechenmeister moved at a speed that permitted him a full day of hard work. At 67 he probably walked no slower than when he took over his father's farm 49 years ago, and, except for the equipment that lessened some of the heavy lifting, he probably worked just as hard. Part of the problem of getting him to part with his farm was that he didn't know any other way. At the door he took off his hat that covered the white top of his head that contrasted with his ruddy wind-blown face. He nodded toward Hazel and George as though it was customary for George to be sitting there with his wife.

George got to his feet and Hazel said, "Herman, come on over and join us. Mr. Roth wants to give us some money."

Mr. Kruechenmeister ambled across the room and grasped George's hand.

"Good to see you again, Mr. K."

The older man didn't answer but he made a noise, a grunt or a hmfff. He looked down at the now empty pie plates and smiled before sitting across from George, under the mirror.

"Your wife makes the best pie I've ever had, as good as my grandmother's. No yours is better," he said to Hazel.

"Now George, don't blaspheme your grandma. Herman, Mr. Roth wants to make us a proposal."

"This is such a beautiful piece of land I want to do something special here. Not just a supermarket and a row of stores. If you'd consider bringing the price down a little, I can build something we'll all be proud of."

Mr. Kruechenmeister listened attentively. He didn't smile, nod or show any other reaction except to glance over George's shoulder at Jesus on the wall.

They sat in silence. For the first time George heard the tick of the grandfather clock. Hazel sat up straight and looked at her husband.

Mr. Kruechenmeister cleared his throat twice. "You know, I seen your car sitting up here, Mr. Roth, and I had almost the same idea you just had, about doing something special. Only my idea didn't include a lower price." He laughed and Hazel and George did also.

"What did you have in mind?" George asked. Experience told him they were about to make a deal or conclude that they never would. Apprehension crept through him over the prospect that after today he might have no project to develop. Then came mini-euphoria at the prospect of being "stuck" with mixed-use in the Arts District.

"First I'm thinking that if we're going to sell you the land we ought to do it now so I don't have to go out and plant all this corn. And then the beans. And then I'm thinking I've always wanted to build a shrine up at the highway, and maybe you could do that for us.

"A coincidence. The other night I dreamt we named your place, 'St. Francis Center.'" George said. "When I woke I knew St. Francis wouldn't fit in a fancy shopping center. Perhaps 'St. Isidor Center,' the patron saint of farming."

"Well, that's just fine as long as you meet our price."

The chance for a deal was sinking, along with the pie, to the bottom of George's stomach. In the mirror disappointment showed on his face. Smile lines had become wrinkles. Mr. K lacked an awareness of what was possible. Or maybe he knew and just didn't want to tell his wife they weren't moving to Florida.

"And finally if we move," and when he said "move," Mr. K's voice broke, "you need to help us with one other thing."

"Glad to if we can?" George said. He bit his lip to hold back his impatience. He had spent hours at the Kruechenmeisters' dining room table, listening to farm stories that had no direction or climax, only seasonal flows, telling his hosts how their beautiful land warranted a special shopping center, teasing the Kruechenmeisters about their three million dollar asking price, enduring their needling over the two-and-half-million price he and Keys had offered. Their talks had gone nowhere.

"You'll need to find a home for Chipper." Mr. Kruechenmeister said. "The Benedictine Monastery would have been perfect, but Father Klugel tells me it would violate their charter. Something about losing their tax exemption if they violate their charter. Sounds like an excuse to me."

Tax exemption. The phrase caught George's attention. The Catholic Church was tax exempt. It was a charity. Why hadn't he thought of it before? In his head he did the math and adjusted some numbers.

"Mr. K, let's take your ideas one at a time. I can picture a prominent shrine at the center."

"I was thinking six foot high," Mr. Kruechenmeister said.

"Six is okay with me," George said, hoping to avoid a contentious issue. "Let's wait for the architect to tell us the exact size. We both want it to be prominent and tasteful."

"How about this here price?" Mr. Kruechenmeister said. "We still need our three million dollars."

"Here's how we'll get you three million," George said. "I'm going to pay you part and I'll reduce your income tax to make up for the rest."

"Don't give me any funny talk," the farmer said. "I also had a dream that I built a Catholic theme park here."

"Herman, that would be wonderful," Mrs. Kruechenmeister said. "We'll make it a drive-through and I'll sell my pies."

"It's not funny talk," George said. "I'll build the shrine but you'll keep the shrine land. After I finish the shopping center, the shrine land will be worth much more than it is today because someone could put up a gas station or a McDonalds. Instead, you give it to the Church and take a tax deduction.

"I want cash, Mr. Roth. Not trouble with the IRS."

"Say I pay you two million five. Wait a second, let me finish." George raised his hand. "If I pay you three million you'll have about two-million-two left after Uncle Sam and the governor take their taxes. Suppose instead I pay you two million five, but you get a million dollar tax deduction by giving the land to the church." George turned his pad of paper sideways so Mr. Kruechenmeister could watch him do the math. "Your taxes are much less. You'll still have the same two-million-two left over after taxes. You don't mind saving taxes, do you?"

"Well no, I kind of like it."

"Here's another idea. We'll fly both of you to Florida now so you can look at houses. Once you change your residence to Florida, you won't have state income tax."

"Florida, now you're talking, George," Mrs. Kreuchenmeister said.

"I don't know about any Florida," Mr. Kreuchenmeister said.

"I'll tell you what," George said. "Do you remember last fall when I explained how we'd have to do some tests on the land, be sure the soil will hold our building, no environmental problems, things like that. Those tests take some time. I'll pay you right now, as soon as we sign a contract, what you would have earned by farming this summer and you won't have to start the tractor except to give me a ride. I'll do the tests. If they're okay, I buy the land and you get the after-tax amount three million would have left you with. If the tests aren't good, which is unlikely, you keep the money I've given you and you've lost nothing by taking the year off. It's probably even good for the land. Furthermore, we'll fly you to Florida this week or whenever you want to take a look. Why don't I have my lawyer draw up a contract?"

"You sit here a moment, Mr. Roth, while I speak with the Missus."

Maybe we have a deal, George thought. The two-million-five price that even Keys is willing to pay. The shrine land would have to be large enough to support a high value, but Keys and he would still have enough land for two or three out lots. He'd need his mother's forgiveness for putting a religious shrine in his shopping center. He'd remind her how she had sent him to Catholic mass with the kid next door so she could have an hour alone on Sunday mornings.

"We'll take your deal," Mr. Kruechenmeister said, "but even with this tax stuff, we want two million seven."

"Two million six is my top dollar," George said. "More than my partner is willing to pay, but if he won't go along, I'll pay the extra out of my share. If that won't do, I have to walk away as much as I love the land and both of you."

Mr. Kruechenmeister raised several details about keeping their house until Thanksgiving. Neither mentioned the future home for Chipper. If Mr. Kruechenmeister persisted and Chipper didn't keel over chasing squirrels, he'd find a home for her.

The farmer held out his hand.

CHAPTER 11

After a couple hours with Mr. Kruechenmeister walking the muddy farm in search of a suitable site for the shrine, George picked up a sandwich and drove home to shower and change for the abortion debate. He had outlined his ideas, anticipated questions and practiced the short, sound-bite answers that talk show hosts permitted. No sniping and name calling, but instead he'd probe for logical common ground. How could anyone object to the idea that parents should be able to choose whether and when to have children?

His charcoal gray suit with the muted stripe, the one he saved for funerals and meetings with bankers, would convey a moderate, sincere attitude. He grabbed a blue shirt and a black and burgundy tie. In between bites from the cucumber, tuna and mustard sandwich, he buttoned the collar and looped the tie.

Bonnie had commandeered the twenty-foot-long black walnut table in the dining room, leaving barely enough space for his notes and sandwich. Books, statistical reports, hospital publicity pamphlets and other indescribable chaos surrounded him. George could see her continuing her research indefinitely as she faced the realities of financing, hiring employees, looking for customers, opening an office, all the rest of the mundane tasks of starting a business. It took revolutionaries like Silicon Valley geniuses and the emerging capitalists in China to bypass bureaucratic red tape and make money.

The mirror at the back door had to do without Bonnie there to straighten his tie and tell him he looked okay. Twice he tried to shift the tie's indentation to just below the base of the knot but couldn't get it right. With one exception, no two, counting his mother, his was a rational world. When it came to his job, his marriage, his children, the temple, people acted reasonably. For example Bonnie wouldn't throw away a lot of money on her new business; she was the most level-headed, common-sense person he knew.

The exception to his logical world was the totally irrational abortion controversy. When he accepted an invitation to join the Family Planning Center board and volunteered for the speaker's bureau, he had two goals: Convince every person in the metropolitan area to have the children they wanted and avoid having an unexpected child. In essence, plan their families with their heads, not their genitals. (At an early meeting he had said "penises" and had been upbraided for assuming that family planning decisions should be made only by males. His archaic choice of words had retarded his acceptance by female board members for more than a year.) His second goal was to develop a dialogue with the Opposition that would lead to a rational compromise. Get away from the emotion. Both goals were failures. In the metropolitan area, couples, some of whom hardly knew each other, many of whom were under eighteen, produced hundreds of unwanted pregnancies a year. And until this afternoon, the Opposition had refused to even sit down with him.

He eased the SAAB out of his side of the garage. In the flow of traffic, he thought of the bomb 5 days ago at the Family Planning Center. His face flushed with anger. SAVE claimed it was non-violent, yet their outrageous protests–blocking doors to abortion clinics, lying down in front of traffic–incited people and encouraged violence. They were as non-violent as setting off a cannon in avalanche country is "harmless." Their goal: Government should mandate that women give birth to unwanted children. He calmed his anger.

In its place came some butterflies in his stomach, the kind that felt good, that told him he was ready. He turned on the radio and pushed the KQQV button. An economist provided a long, technical answer to a caller's simple question.

A billboard along the highway said, "God is Pro Life." Susan Cordry could be difficult. Before becoming an activist she had been a socialite, a fixture at the annual, debutante coming-out ball. People had laughed when, with debutante demeanor, she had delivered to the Speaker of the United States House of Representatives petitions in support of a law to prohibit mothers from working outside the home until all their children were in school. A national news magazine had carried her picture on its cover when she had led demonstrations in Washington to exclude women from equal rights protections. People stopped laughing when the Supreme Court agreed.

Abortion was now her target. God told Susan Cordry a fetus was a human being. No one else's God mattered. God had not spoken to George, but he could rationally present the issues. If he could turn down the volume, more people would opt for tolerance. This fantasy so distracted him that he scraped his front bumper against the curved wall on the downtown garage's circular ramp.

Walking down six flights of stairs used up some energy and helped to calm him. A strong wind had chased a brief shower to the east, leaving a fresh feel to the air. He J-walked across the street along with a blown newspaper page that wrapped around the trunk of a pear tree.

When he turned the corner at the office building that housed KQQV, a mob stared back at him. At least twice as many demonstrators as he had ever seen in front of the abortion clinic. They overflowed the sidewalk and occupied half of the one-way street in front of the building, not unlike a crowd of teenagers waiting for the door to open for a rock concert. A slew of cars pouring off the southbound freeway to reach the central business district backed up at the funnel point. "Babies yes, murder no," the crowd chanted at the request of a diminutive, gray-suited woman with a clipboard and bullhorn.

The blast of voices shook George and almost pushed him back around the corner. The crowd was ugly. They jammed together. He wished he could avoid them, but knew he had to step forward. He didn't panic. Instead he walked toward the mass of bodies. One step at a time. There was no alternative. No turning back. Besides, these sycophants didn't represent middle America, the people who would listen on the radio. Zealous demonstrators would not deprive him of his chance.

"Let the murderer through," screamed the gray-suited woman. "Come ahead, Mr. Roth. We're exercising our freedom of speech. You're not against freedom of speech, are you?"

Her congregants laughed. A passage opened as two people in front of him moved a foot and a half apart. They must have been thirty feet deep. Faces blurred like in the shrouded background in a Rembrandt painting. He clamped his lips and moved forward.

Arms and legs along the narrow human chute brushed against him. The crowd compressed, momentarily blocked him, and then separated so he could take the next step, like a mouse inside a ravenous snake. Finally he emerged from the mass. The door that would revolve him to safety beckoned twenty feet ahead. He walked slowly, unintimidated, relishing his victory. As he entered the V of the revolving door, someone behind him said, "Mr. Roth," spoken like the speaker was about to follow with a question. Should he turn back? His head said yes, his body said keep going. "Mr. Roth." The voice shouted. "Look here." It was a man and the words were a challenge. George turned, barely in time to flinch from a thrown object, the size of a football. He raised his hand to protect his face. The object thudded into his palm. With a start he realize he had grabbed a large, close-to-term fetus. It felt real. And even though it couldn't be real, without thinking, he cradled it against his body.

Yes, it seemed like a baby. What should he do? No time to think. Two men ran toward him. They carried a bucket, like one of those containers football players use to drench the coach. He backed into the door's vortex but couldn't get away. Together the two men hurled. Their aim was wild, but because he now stood in front of two glass walls, the contents that missed him splashed down his back. He was soaked and when he looked down at his gray suit and blue shirt, he realized he was soaked with blood.

George had kept his cool with the doll. He assumed it was a doll because no one would throw a real fetus. He would never know for certain if it were real because when he had raised his arms to ward off the blood, the doll had slipped to the pavement and someone had picked it up. He handled the blood okay too. That is, until it oozed through his shirt and his undershirt and matted to the hair on his chest, making him think it was his own blood. From his mouth came a sound whose origin he didn't know. It wasn't from his throat. It wasn't from his lungs. The scream came from the depth of his darkest wound.

He pushed as hard as he could to his left against the revolving door but it didn't budge. A man on the inside was pushing to the right against him. The mob had him trapped in the door. The danger snapped back his self-control. He turned toward them, paused a moment as he took in the staring faces. Then let loose with a different kind of scream. A controlled scream he had learned 30 years earlier from a sergeant in Army ROTC who was teaching bayonet fighting. The noise was designed to frighten aggressors (the Army's generic name for the opposition). "Shock 'em back on their heels," the sergeant had demanded, "and then slice 'em open. Kill or be killed." George had wondered if he could slice someone open. Not having a bayonet, he bent into a crouch and brought up his open hands like a karate fighter he had seen in the movies.

It worked. The throng backed away. Two faces right in front of him turned from amusement to fear. The front row retreated, forcing back the laughing, poster-waving people behind them. Several stumbled, some cried out. George turned his back to show a matador's arrogance. A guard was waving him into the building, the same man who had pushed the door against him.

Inside the guard said, "I was trying to open the door for you. Is your name Roth?" He was dressed in a uniform and seemed hesitant as he glanced at his clipboard. He was the sentry who had awakened after the war.

"I'm George Roth." Adrenalin pushed his words into an unfamiliar voice. "I'm on the three o'clock call-in program. Despite this mob, I'm ready."

CHAPTER 12

The guard showed George the way to KQQV's private elevator. Thankfully alone, George rose thirty-eight stories to the studio. A mirror at the back of the elevator revealed a dark stain across the front of his suit. His shirt bore the monogram of a "v" where his buttoned jacket had left it exposed. When he was sixteen, he changed shirts because of a spec on the front. Today he didn't care.

Just off the elevator, Susan Cordry sat on a straight back chair in the reception area.

"Mr. Roth, I just heard. I'm so sorry," she said as she stood up. Tall and sparse with powdered skin, she was dressed for high tea in a Wedgwood green suit. "I hope you're not injured."

"You're as sorry as when you unlawfully block an abortion clinic." He regretted that he couldn't control his anger

"I beg your pardon, Mr. Roth. SAVE deplores violence and certainly the treatment you received."

"Like the bomb last week at the Family Planning Center."

The studio door opened, and a man walked out. "I'm Keith Roberts," the call-in host said in his rhythmic radio voice. He was short and hefty, nothing like George imagined from listening to him on the radio. "Seven minutes of news, then we're on. But if you want, Mr. Roth, we can reschedule. In fact Ms. Cordry even suggested it."

George insisted on going ahead. For an hour, minus commercials, news, weather, sports and traffic, he and Cordry ping-ponged the usual pro-choice—pro-life arguments the country had heard for forty years. At one point while Cordry droned on, George yanked himself out of an image of having sex with her. This cruel mind trick almost made him sick.

Afterwards on the ride down the elevator, Cordry said, "SAVE doesn't forget."

"Sounds like a threat."

"Perhaps, but not of violence."

Walking to the car he couldn't shake a mild anxiety from having lost control when he had screamed at the mob. During the debate he had accused Cordry of caring about the unborn but not caring about living human beings. Where was her support for family leave, childcare for working parents?

That night friends and supporters called and congratulated him for his "victory." He felt validated. Even his mother said, "You are passionate about something. On to Paris."

Over the weekend Herman Kreuchenmeister also called. He left a voicemail message at George's office that the deal was off because he wasn't going to sell his farm to an abortionist.

"What do we do now, Sport," Keys said Monday morning as George walked into Keys' office.

"You need to go see them," George said. "Tell them they don't have to deal with me." The muscles in his chest tensed. He liked the Kreuchenmeisters and regretted causing them angst. Still, Keys had charmed more than one farmer and could get the deal done.

"I'm afraid they'll demand that you're not part of the deal. Not even a silent owner." Inside Keys' credenza a CD droned, a dreary piece, maybe Shostakovich. "What'll we do then, Slugger?"

"That's not really their business," George said.

Keys scrolled through his smartphone that contained all the information he needed to run his business. Notes filled the calendar slots allotted each day. Like December 26 listed the people to whom he wanted to send thankyous, reminding George that Keys would begin with, "Dolores, prepare a letter to Dolores Simpson. Dear Dolores. Thanks so much," and so forth. One year Dolores typed the letter and added, "Dolores, enclosed is your $10,000 New Year's bonus."

"Maybe we should each do a different deal. Are you still thinking about the Arts District."

"Thinking but far from deciding."

Keys glanced at his phone, and George assumed they were proceeding through his agenda. "What if we go our separate ways. I'll take over Kreuchenmeister and you do the Arts District or any other deal you want. It's not like either of us needs more deals to get by. You could work for the Family Planning Center for a dollar a year."

George was stunned. He had no great financial or personal need to continue his partnership with Keys. Yet all at once he realized the power of his own inertia. While he had the knowledge and ability to do deals on his own, he had become accustomed to Keys' charm and charisma leading the way. George then took the steps to get the shopping centers approved and built.

But could he be the catalyst? Could he imagine the pieces for the Arts District and then put them together? Was he an entrepreneur? Did he want to be an entrepreneur? Was he afraid of trying and failing?

"Think it over and then let's talk."

George already liked the idea. He struggled to recall some of the good times they had experienced together. The enjoyment of working with Keys was in the past. Maybe this was true of many successful businesses. Youth and the challenge of getting established provided pleasure. Success provided money and prominence, which are great but not as gratifying.

"I will think it over."

"We can both work out of this building," Keys said, "Though we'd need a separation arrangement for the office and the shopping centers."

"Like what?"

"Either one of us can name a price. Then the other

chooses whether to buy or sell at that price. The initiator needs to name an honest price because he doesn't know whether he'll be the buyer or seller."

"Sounds like a pre-nuptial agreement. We've done fine without separation agreements." George said. "Why complicate it now."

"Suppose you get brave and do the Arts District deal. I don't want you pledging your half of our shopping centers with a bank in order to obtain a loan. If you get in trouble, the bank'll move in and I'll end up with Spencer Elliot Smith or some other unimaginative vice president trying to tell me how to run my business."

"The same could happen to you with the Kruechenmeister deal. Either one of us might need to pledge his interest."

"Right, it goes both ways," Keys said. "What happens if you want to spend money on your deal while I want cash to take a bimbo to the Caribbean. We need an arrangement now in case we can't settle our differences later."

"Your "name-a-price" deal is unfair if one of us has cash and the other doesn't."

"Keep your money handy."

"I might need cash for a new deal and not have it handy." Was Keys setting him up? "Your 'name-a-price' works if whoever initiates must name a price for each property separately. The other one of us can buy or sell all or buy some and sell some projects, have sale proceeds both coming in and going out." George figured he'd be the responder and could either sell all or sell some to provide cash to buy the others. He'd never initiate this procedure unless he already had the financing.

"I'll think about that." Keys half nodded, half shook his head before he disappeared into the kitchen. He returned with another glass of water and some protein powder. Something to build his body or improve his sex life. Last month it was bee pollen.

"What have you got there?" George asked.

"Something for my pecs."

"That stuff's dangerous."

"Nah." Keys flushed a heaping tablespoon of the powder down with a full glass of water. Now and then George fretted that despite his own clean living, Keys would find some way, some perversion of science, to live longer than he.

"One more thing," Keys said. "As long as we're partners I'd like to continue to manage the centers." Keys explained why, but George's mind wandered. He didn't care about managing their shopping centers. Keys might screw him a little here or there, but nickel and dime advantages had never been his thing. George would rather spend time helping the Family Planning Center, which reminded him of his next meeting with Sheila Szabo.

"What do you say?" Keys asked presumably about managing shopping centers.

"Let's try it. We can go to an independent manager if either of us thinks it's not working."

"Sounds good, Tiger." Keys set down his phone. Presumably they had reached the end of his list.

"It's noon," Keys said. "I have my weekly appointment at the barber shop. You want to join me? Saul's razor might make you a handsome man."

George declined.

CHAPTER 13

Emanuel Brown's office was in a brick building with a glass front, the only un-boarded glass in the block. During college George had worked a summer job in a nearby warehouse. For lunch back then he'd grabbed an apple and a package of Twinkies at a neighborhood shop, played stick ball in the street, and dodged water from fire hydrants opened to fight the heat. Today, with no one in sight, the neighborhood conveyed a sense of hostile abandonment.

A receptionist using a telephone headset gestured George toward the back. He walked through a large expanse with only one desk where Binta sat in front of an iMac. She waved him toward the open door to Brown's office, where Brown sat behind an old oak desk, signing checks. His sweatshirt and overalls contrasted with the gray suit, button-down shirt and paisley tie he wore in a large photo of a hospital groundbreaking that hung on the wall behind him. Without standing, he motioned George to a seat.

"Estelle says you want to do some business. Estelle," he shouted. "Join us."

"Estelle?" George said.

"Binta, Dad. My name's Binta," she said as she walked in and sat next to George in front of her father.

"Call yourself what you want. I'll use your real name."

"Why 'Binta?'" George said.

"George, you're a cultural illiterate. Binta Kinte was Kunta Kinte's mother. Ever hear of Roots?"

"Of course."

"Estelle calls herself Binta because supposedly all life sprang from Binta Kinte. You have a daughter, Roth?"

George nodded and smiled.

"My daughter from whom all life springs thinks I should retire and let her take over."

"Estelle may need a few years' experience to take over," George said, "but she's already a great sales… salesperson."

"She must be to interest you in my Grand Avenue property." Brown leaned back, hands behind his head until the telephone cut him short. "Yes." He listened for thirty seconds with his eyes on George's. Lines around his mouth tightened. Then in a menacing voice, he said, "Look man. You tell that mothah to wrap the shit or we'll hang his ass from his crane. Get back on that job or he can forget workin' in the city. Ever. You hear? You better hear. Now get out there and tell 'im." Brown's voice pushed George back in his chair. He pictured some guy hanging from a crane. Contractors building George's shopping centers had expressed similar directives, but with not quite such clarity. He shifted in his chair and looked away from Brown and then back again.

Brown gently set down the phone. "Excuse me, Roth." He spoke in his previous voice. "Construction's not an easy business. Where were we? Oh yes, Estelle is an excellent salesman."

"She sees your property as a cornerstone for a mixed-use development in the Arts District." George tried to relax. Over the years he had walked into countless rooms where he knew no one, where some people wondered who the hell he was. He had courted national retailers in plush suites in large cities. He hadn't been nervous when he probably should have been. Getting together with Emmanuel Brown not only differed from past experience, but stirred feelings that troubled him, that ran counter to expectations and perhaps showed biases.

"Estelle has big ideas." Brown smiled. "That's fine, Sweetheart, especially as long as I'm around with a dose of reality. But you both need some history before you invade the city."

"At first," Brown continued, "Black people weren't allowed to live in the heart of the city which was a few blocks from the Mississippi River. So the whites shoved us into a swamp twenty blocks west. Then the white folk decided they'd push us out, fill in the swamp and move in, so they passed some laws, took away our property, and bludgeoned us north and further west. That's how my family got the land where my building is. That was okay for families like yours, Roth, because you moved to the suburbs to get away from us. But then you decide to save gasoline or whatever and moved back to the city. While you were at it, you decided it would be nice to have an Arts District. That's fine. I doubt if your Arts District took much of our property. In fact you brought business to my parking lots. But your mixed-use project, that's another story."

"Is it possible?"

"A mixed-use development might be good for white people in the city, maybe even for Black people. At a reasonable price, I'd throw in my building. But now we're a majority in the city. The city isn't going to allow you to push us around like before."

"All our shopping centers are in communities where you can't push people around. It's always us who get pushed around."

"People here will oppose you just because they have nothing better to do. Some will want a bribe."

"We've run into that. We don't pay."

"You'd need a partner who knows the city."

"Dad, let's do it with George. We'll be sure it's done right and learn a new business."

"Estelle, I'm a contractor with six projects underway. I'm not about to chase a fantasy."

"The largest shopping center developer in the country began business as a building contractor," George said.

"And another ten went broke."

"I could work with George," Binta said. "I graduate in December. I'd learn more than in business school."

"What about my marketing?" Brown said.

"She could do both," George said. "You're right. Every development is a fantasy without months of investigation and planning before a developer commits much money. One of our deals required 3 years and a referendum to get township approval. Pre-development won't be full time for me and needn't be for Bin-- Estelle."

Partnering with the Brown family would be a tremendous advantage. He had checked 4 different references on Emanuel Brown. All came back positive with the warning that he could be difficult to negotiate with. All the better for a partner. Working with Binta would be a lot more fun than Harry Keys these days.

"Fine with me. George, if you want Estelle for a partner?" George sensed that Brown and Binta had discussed this earlier. She didn't care for business school and probably wasn't excited to work construction. "Just remember. This isn't two-four or four-one."

"Two-four, four-one?"

"Zip codes, George. West County zip codes."

"Got it." George smiled, which Brown didn't reciprocate.

"One more thing," Brown said. "Estelle will be on my payroll, but I want a share of any development you go ahead with. And I want to be the general contractor."

"No problem with either," George said. He'd be delighted to have Brown as his partner and would gladly give up 50% if he had to, which right now was 50% of nothing. The real questions, assuming they actually did a development, were how they shared liabilities and decision-making as well as the amount of the construction fee. From experience he knew that generosity made success more likely. Half of a success was preferable to all of nothing. "Do you want to write up something for me to sign?"

Brown got to his feet and held out his hand. "A handshake works for me," he said. The meeting was over. The contractor walked him to his car, waving to a passerby. As George drove west, he wondered if he had gone too far with Emanuel Brown whom he hardly knew. Still all projects were speculative, this one more than most. Part of his decision to commit would depend on his relationship with Brown. Without Kreuchenmeister, what else did he have to do? As Keys said, he could always become a full-time volunteer, but he wasn't ready to retire.

CHAPTER 14

Sheila called because Debbie had a fever. "I might need to take her to the doctor, so let's reschedule unless you want to plan the kickoff at my place tomorrow."

At 8:30 he rang the bell. No response. The large house in an older subdivision reminded him of the days when buyers weren't concerned with conservation. He rang again and then walked across the lawn to the driveway to look for a car. Maybe she had taken Debbie to the doctor, or worse, to the hospital.

No car, but as he debated what to do, Sheila's Audi zipped down the street and turned into the driveway.

"I left the door unlocked," she said through the lowering window. With a grocery bag in one arm, she hopped out and kissed him on the cheek like they had been married for years. She hooked his arm and walked him across the lawn. "Debbie is so much better I took her to school and stopped for some muffins on the way home. Come on in."

He followed her through the front hall, the dining room and into the kitchen, unable to avoid observing how her jeans snuggled around her butt. Sheila and he alone at her house triggered fantasies, which with his self-control intact, felt safe.

"Grab some coffee and let's go out back," she said. They sat at a picnic table on a patio that covered half the yard. A mixture of scents wafted from the other half which consisted of a lawn, three rows of daffodils, a variety of succulents, and a hot tub. Mature pines shielded them from an adjacent country-club golf course. Sheila's ubiquitous legal pad on the table inspired an image of her developing solutions for a hospital's problems.

"What does your former husband do?" he asked admiring the house and landscaping.

"He teaches English at the University." With a smirk on her face, she said, "For a supposed feminist, you're a sexist. My consulting business paid for this. Let's get started."

She took him through her notes. "After the clinic tour we'll take the solicitors to the board room. That's the key moment. We have to rev up some excitement. Try this." She broke off a piece of a blueberry muffin, and pushed it into his mouth, holding out a finger for him to lick some icing. "Here are some choices," she said. "We find some clients willing to tell their stories."

"But—"

"No, wait. Here's another idea. We show a film, one of the 'Teen Monologues' with two teenagers talking about how they were making out, saying 'no' like they really meant it, all the while getting hotter and hotter until saying no didn't work. Or, a third possibility, we do a gestalt on being an unwanted child."

"A what?"

"A gestalt exercise. We role play. Solicitors imagine and act out being an unwanted child. I'd start, as an example, and then we'd ask for volunteers."

"Sounds weird. Have you don't that."

"I go on personal retreats to better understand myself and my place in the world. One time the leader taught gestalt exercises. What do you think?"

What did he think? He'd like to gestalt the Teen Monologue film with Sheila right now. He stifled the thought. Was he an unwanted child? His mother had been unprepared for single motherhood when his father had gone to Viet Nam. He was 5 years old at the time and remembered no details from back then, only a need to make his mother happy. Usually unsuccessful.

"They're all good."

"The least risky is the first, the client stories. But I think the gestalt would be more fun, more exciting. Want to try it?"

"Go ahead, show me."

"I'll pretend you're my mother," she said.

Sheila sat straight in her wire-backed chair, eyes closed. When she opened them, she stared at George and began a barely audible monologue. "When you had me, Mom, you didn't want me. You made me lie in my dirty diapers. You shoved a bottle into my mouth. No soft breast. You screamed at me when I cried. You dropped me into my crib. I was afraid you'd throw me against the wall if I cried too much, but I had to cry to get fed." Her voice gradually rose after the hot tub heater and circulator started up. "When I got older you made me stay in my room. You didn't look after me. You never read to me. If I complained you took away my two toys, the stuffed bunny the cat had torn apart, and the headless Barbie. You should have given me a heartless Barbie," As she spit out the words, she rose to her feet and walked toward him. "I hate you," she screamed. Then she stopped and looked down into his eyes with a big grin. "Made up and exaggerated, but you get the idea? In a true gestalt, you'd play my mother and respond."

George let out a deep breath. "Would people feel uncomfortable?"

"Damn right. That's how they should feel about unwanted children."

"I agree. But will all that emotion teach them how to make a reasoned sales pitch?"

"George, you don't run your shopping centers based on reason. You create an atmosphere that makes people want to buy, shell out their money. Fund raising is no different. Give it a try." She reached for his hand and pulled him up so they stood face to face.

He thought again of his mother, then and now. Her fragile body, her great spirit. He didn't want to attack her regardless of back then. He made excuses for other people's mistakes, and struggled to forgive his own.

"My mother pretty much left me to raise myself after the army called up my father."

"Pretend I'm her. Tell me."

Instead he reached for Sheila's shoulders, pulled her toward him and kissed her. A soft quiet kiss. For a moment he rationalized he was play acting, a gestalt. Then her mouth opened and her tongue worked its way to his. Make believe was no longer possible.

Their hips came together. The kiss became passionate. His body strained against hers, hers against his. Then Sheila stepped back. "Since that first afternoon," she said, "we've both wanted to fuck. No, don't answer, I feel it and know it. It's wonderful. But it's not like your marriage is falling apart. At least not yet. You need to decide, when we're not in such teenage form."

She was right. This wasn't a college hook up with someone he might or might not see again. He was infatuated, too soon to say he was in love, maybe falling in love. He and Bonnie had hardly seen each other the past few weeks, she so occupied with her business, he with his usual full days, sometimes evenings. For several years their marriage had become a benevolent routine, while they slowly grew apart. Aware of other couples who had given up on what seemed like at least an okay marriage, they had gone to a counselor who described their lives as "a good hamburger stand of a marriage." Giving it energy required more effort, which neither seemed committed to give.

He stood there looking into Sheila's dark brown eyes, aware of a soft breeze, the chlorine in the hot tub, the distant crack of a golf shot, someone saying, "nice drive," a robin singing.

"I've thought about it," he said, "but I need to buy some condoms."

"No problem. I use a diaphragm—you can insert it." She

laughed, and pulled him toward the house.

⇋

Two hours later — he knew the time when the Civil
Defense air-raid sirens sounded their noon, first-Monday-of
the-month test — he lay in Sheila's bed watching nymph-
like shadows dance on the ceiling as breeze-blown, sheer
white drapes darted in and floated out an open window. His
thoughts ricocheted between the pleasures of Sheila and
the betrayal of Bonnie. Did an affair make sense? If Bonnie
found out, could she live with the pain and he the shame?

When Sheila stirred and rolled on to her side toward
him, he said, "I'm not sure what we've done?"

"You're the only board member of the Family Planning
Center who could wonder what we've done." Her laugh
excited him. He struggled for control.

Her face was a foot from his, her hand lightly stroking
his chest. He relished sensual Sheila, master of the sexual
gestalt, who had carried him somewhere he had never been
and then kept him there while she had moaned. He lay there
thinking of his betrayal while at the same time, he relished
touching Sheila, covering every millimeter of her body with
his lips and tongue.

Sheila gave him a lingering kiss, no less sensual than
earlier. She rolled onto her back and sighed as she stretched
her arms above her head. He tried to roll on top of her, but
she jumped out of bed ahead of him and gave his cock a

squeeze on her way to the bathroom.

"You can use the shower while I'm in the tub," she called.

First he picked up his phone. He had missed some calls and an emergency text from Harry Keys. "I've been looking all over for you. A problem at the Kruechenmeister farm. Call me immediately."

CHAPTER 15

"Antiquities," Keys said. "The engineers at the farm found some graves."

"You sound out of breath. Are you okay?"

"I'm on the treadmill at the gym. I'm fine even though every time I get on this thing, I'm afraid I'll kill myself."

"Take it easy. What kind of graves?" George said.

"Indian, I think. This could crater the whole deal."

"What will you do?"

"I need your help."

"Harry, it's your deal. I'm glad to discuss it, but I've got my hands full at the moment." Sheila stifled a laugh as she walked by naked on the way to the tub.

"Like you said, if I get in trouble in this deal, it could affect our other properties. Meet me at the office tomorrow. It won't take much of your time."

"Eight o'clock. I volunteer at the food pantry at ten."

My life's insane, George thought. He rubbed what smelled like lavender soap over his body as though he could clean away the mess. The Kruechenmeisters want a shrine, and a home for Chipper, their dog. Instead they end up with a cemetery. Next they'll want a kennel. He found a towel without bothering Sheila who was asleep or meditating in the tub. Drying himself, he wondered how Keys would get rid of the bones.

As he dressed, he watched Sheila run a towel over her

body, her shapely breasts. He had the strangest thought: Would he and Sheila have had a dull, routine marriage if they had married twenty years ago? Would he be attracted to Bonnie with her large bouncy boobs? Having an affair seemed inevitable. He liked Sheila, her laugh, her smell. He admired that she ran her own business while raising a daughter. All at once he felt ashamed. How could moral upstanding George Roth, past president of Temple Isaiah, relish adultery? Spending the day fucking, fucking up. He had to stop gaping at Sheila's boobs.

"You have a great house," he said as he tied his shoes.

"Far too big. I ought to sell it, but I'm afraid my husband might try to get custody of Debbie, and my lawyer says keeping the house strengthens my case."

"He might have a detective watching you. Watching us right now."

She waved the thought away. "Don't worry, he knows my office is here and that I meet with people here." He wished she'd put on her clothes.

"He'd love to have pictures for the judge. We'd be courtroom porn stars."

She grinned and laughed, loud enough he feared, that they could hear her on the golf course. "You're a very funny man," she said. Finally she pulled on her panties. "Picture the courtroom."

"I have. A bunch of lawyers watching. Reruns on the ten o'clock news."

"I can see it too," she said. "The screen blinks, a blizzard at first, and then you and me, honey, the skin stars of the twenty-first century." She laughed louder.

He cringed.

"Sometimes he talks custody, but Debbie spends a lot of time with him already." She rubbed some cream on her belly and breasts. "Relax. Next time we'll lock the doors."

Next time? Sheila and he fucking the summer away. Excitement ran chills down his back and his cock started to grow. Could he handle an affair? The lies, the made-up meetings, the jealous husband fighting for custody of his daughter, and Bonnie. He and Bonnie had sex every few weeks. Would fucking Sheila twice that morning make him unable to get a hard on?

She walked over to where he stood and circled her arms around him. "You wanted this the moment you stepped in my front door." She kissed him, and he reached around to her naked back and held her tight. "If I saw it so clearly, you couldn't have hidden it from yourself."

"This deal is driving me crazy," Keys said. "I'm trying to do the stuff you usually do, while I guess you're fumbling around the city doing what I'm good at."

"I learned a lot of the business from you. I'm sure you can handle some bones. If not, your contract with the Kreuchenmeisters gives you an out."

"I lost my temper yesterday after the engineer brought in

some tribal representative I have to deal with. Your buddy, Mrs. Kreuchenmeister, insists I get you involved."

"Mr. K thinks I'm an abortionist and doesn't want me around."

"Guess who makes the decisions on the farm."

George thought about the women in his life, Bonnie, Sheila, Binta, his mother, and now Mrs. K. All strong women, even Bonnie these days.

"Do the Kreuchenmeisters know whose bones they are?"

"Mr. Kruechenmeister says his family has owned this place since the 1890's. These are from way before then."

"Now what?" George asked.

"Hart, the engineer, has dealt with this before and says I'm in for delays. How long depends on dealing with the Indians, which is what I need you to do."

"Might help to say "Native Americans" instead of "Indians.""

"Whatever."

Always put the relationship ahead of the problem, George had learned. Building some personal capital with Harry Keys was a good idea. He had the time so he agreed to meet at the farm with the Native American representative.

⇆

"Here comes the lawyer," cried out a woman as George entered the courtyard at St. Vincent de Paul Cathedral. The

Cathedral ran a foodbank where he had volunteered with the Catholic Legal Ministry once a month since he was in law school. He had never practiced law but continued to do intakes. While St. Vincent had once been the center of the Arch Diocese, currently it was more mission than church. The Archbishop had moved the power and pomp to the fashionable midtown where it was one of the anchors for the part of the city where the Arts District was located.

"I'll be ready for you, Ginger," he said to the woman who had called out his arrival. He wove through the crowd, mostly women, huddled together for warmth, waiting for the April sun to clear the steeple. How could people so short on food and long on challenges be so cheerful?

Inside he wound down the basement stairs to the ancient gym. Meola Martinez, who ran the operation, announced: "Anyone needs help with the bill collector, landlord, stuff like that, sign up for the lawyer." Her Spanish lilt wafted over the hubbub.

He poured a cup of coffee and took a minute to glance through the handouts Meola distributed for the church.

"Take your coffee and I'll send in the clients," she said.

"What's the rush?"

"I'm showing these young mothers how to use condoms." She held up a rubber and a zucchini. "Move along unless you want to demonstrate."

Aglow, he fled the laughter to his office in the former men's locker room. There he encountered the Monsignor, who sat at George's desk. "I had to find somewhere to avoid the blasphemy," the retired cleric said.

"A priest has difficult choices these days."

"Not as difficult as the flock."

For a moment George wondered how effective Sheila's diaphragm was. Maybe a rubber would be safer.

In the makeshift office he straightened the chairs and drew a legal pad from his briefcase before his first client walked in. For the next couple hours he scribbled tales of past due debts, black and blue marriages and evicted families. He solved some problems with a phone call, stepping over the line that required a law license. A woman named Hilda sobbed and moaned. "The sheriff put us onto the street, my children, the baby, all our furniture."

"Terrible," he said. "Where are they now?"

"My husband who's laid off stayed with the children. A policeman is already telling them to move on. He called a truck to haul away our stuff."

George called Molly Ponce, his Legal Ministry "boss," and found her waiting outside a courtroom for the next of her twelve cases on the day's docket. "Probably nothing I can do, George. I'll call the sheriff to try for more time."

George thanked her and added, "I'm working on a project in the Arts District and I wonder if you could introduce me to the Archbishop for a short meeting to get his feel. The project is part affordable housing, which relates to the terrible condition this poor family is in."

"I can," Molly said. "Give me a call later and tell me more."

George told Hilda to ask Meola for help with money for housing.

CHAPTER 16

George assumed his jaw-ache was some kind of punishment for adultery. Occasionally it felt like Muhammed Ali had caught him with a right hook. He tried to ignore it but when the pain spread to his ear, he went to an otolaryngologist who found nothing and sent him to the dentist. The dentist diagnosed something George couldn't pronounce. "TMJ will do," the dentist said as she removed the bib from around George's neck. Bonnie's home-remedy book said the best relief from TMJ came from hot towels, soft food, stifled yawns and patience. He wondered whether oral sex with Sheila would help or hurt.

For years George and Bonnie had gone out to dinner on Saturday nights, often with friends. "How about getting together with the Gordons?" he asked when he found Bonnie immersed in notebooks and papers at the black walnut table late one Saturday afternoon.

She looked at him, or perhaps through him, as though his words hadn't registered. George was shocked at her appearance. A calm self-possessed expression. She looked younger. Lines around her eyes had softened. She was full of color. "George, I'm sorry. I had something on my mind. Dinner? I can't. I want to hire two physical therapists, and the only time they could get together is tonight, so I'm taking them to Rodeo's. You're welcome to join us."

"Physical therapists? I thought you were doing home

nursing."

"That was a couple weeks ago. Hugh Collins is so excited about my business plan he suggested I form a limited liability company and expand the services."

"Who's Hugh Collins?"

"The head of CHMO. He thinks my plan will make a real dent in medical costs and provide better service."

"What's CHMO?"

"You need to test your memory. City-County Health Maintenance Organization."

This conversation sounded familiar, as though they had had it before. He couldn't remember. "How'd you get involved with the head of CHMO?" He regretted the words as soon as they left his mouth, certain they would antagonize Bonnie and begin an evening-long battle.

"Isn't that something?" was all she said.

He didn't want to go to Rodeo's with physical therapists. The only time he had been to a physical therapist was after mysteriously acquiring acute back pain. The therapist kept hounding him to stand differently from how he had stood on two feet all his life. He was afraid if he didn't go to dinner, he'd go to Sheila's and slide further away from Bonnie. At least he was able to enjoy his favorite sausage pizza while listening to how the therapists got people off their asses to exercise. Bonnie offered fifteen percent more pay than they'd been receiving. At that rate she'd employ every health provider in town.

⇆

Tuesday George waited for Binta at Starbuck's to plan their morning meeting with Linda Taylor, the president of the University. Taylor had risen to the top, academically and administratively.

"A dry cappuccino," Binta ordered before she sat at the table and pulled a legal pad from a thin briefcase. Her charcoal jacket over a beige blouse and white pants conveyed a presence in the business world. He couldn't recall the clothes his wife wore these days as she pursued her new business. They seldom got home at the same time, and both were quick to put on something casual when they got there.

He was about to comment on Binta's striking appearance but realized that he never noticed what men wore to meetings. He didn't consider himself a sexist, yet consciously wanted to avoid comments that had seemed natural earlier in his life. After she returned with her drink, he said, "What's on your list?"

"Advantages for the University."

"Good preparation," he said as he read the list that included one advantage he hadn't considered.

"George, I've got to get away from construction. You have no idea what it's like to work for my father. Maybe I'll do this real estate stuff. It's mostly common sense."

The aroma from the cinnamon on Binta's cappuccino mixed with George's scant memories of his own father.

Working for a strong father like Emanuel Brown could challenge her pursuit of an identity.

"What are we trying to accomplish in the meeting?" he asked.

"Get Linda Taylor on board."

"At the very least she can't be an opponent."

At the University a receptionist escorted them to Taylor's office where Taylor gestured them to take a seat in front of her desk. Right off the bat, she thanked George for his past gifts to the University. She must know that his contributions had been moderate. That was about to change. He appreciated her skill at informing him of this without asking.

"How is your father?" Taylor asked Binta. "I'm sure he's proud that you're about to graduate from the business school."

"Not that he'd tell me. He's ready to hire me as a laborer."

"Start at the bottom. Not a bad idea. Please tell me what the two of you have in mind by a 'mixed-use project' you mentioned on the phone, George."

Taylor's office projected her authority. She could look out at the University's main quadrangle. Her desk was uncluttered. On the walls several abstract paintings mixed with others that looked like they had been done by her children in elementary school. A trophy sat on a table along with a small exhibit celebrating the University's nine NCAA soccer championships a half century earlier.

George described an integrated project consisting of

housing, office, retail, restaurants, perhaps a hotel along with public places where people could gather both inside and outside like a small park or two. Uses would complement the culture the University had already brought to this part of the city.

"It's a beautiful April morning," Taylor said. "How about if we walk a few blocks north on Grand Avenue so you can show me what might be."

Out on the street, Binta said, "My dream would be to integrate some of our uses with the University. A hotel for your visitors is an obvious example. Someday as you expand, students might want our housing, or you might want to take over part for students."

"Possibly," Taylor said.

"Also," Binta said, "we could consider a shared facility like a small performing arts venue or a business resource center. Business people can use the resources and interact with the students."

"Like? Tell me more."

"A new entrepreneur could consult a library on how to put together a business plan, and brainstorm with students. Established companies could do the same when they want to add a new business."

"Good ideas. No wonder you're carrying a 4.0 at the business school."

George considered the contrast between the somewhat outrageous, expressive Binta Brown when they met at the Bull Market Lounge, and her restrained, business-like manner with Taylor. Taylor's awareness of Binta's GPA showed her added preparation for this meeting, perhaps a hint of her interest in their project.

"What can I do?" Taylor asked.

"We'd want your approval before building in this area, plus your suggestions as we go along," George said.

"I give you my approval," Taylor said. "We'd need to see some plans and layouts to be sure we complement each other."

She'd make a good real estate developer—appear to agree while maintaining control.

They walked back and parted outside the administration building. Walking to their cars, George said, "Not much done, but a necessary step. Your shared facility idea is a good one, though from experience, I doubt the University will contribute to the costs. That's okay but she won't be the last to ask for free goodies. The City and perhaps the Archdiocese and others will have their ideas. A project can usually handle a reasonable request, but too many can kill a project."

CHAPTER 17

A phone call from Harry Keys roused George out of bed at six in the morning. "I'm conferencing you in with Mr. Kreuchenmeister," Keys said. "We have a problem."

"Mr. Keys, I got Indians in my corn field." Herman Kruechenmeister spoke at twice his usual speed. He was angry. "Are you there, Mr. Keys?"

"I'm here, Mr. Kreuchenmeister, along with George Roth."

"You don't own this land yet and Indians weren't part of our deal."

"What are they doing?" Keys asked.

"They're sitting around the bones. I want them off my land. Now."

They heard some muffled conversation, and then Mrs. Kreuchenmeister. "George, we need you to come too."

"We'll both be right there," Keys said. " George, I'll pick you up in 20 minutes."

"I got two hours' sleep," Keys said as they drove to the farm in his Mercedes. "A cold shower hardly helped," as confirmed by a somewhat blotched shave.

Most of the traffic was headed downtown, the opposite direction. "If my head didn't feel like a bowling ball after an all-night tourney, and if these Indians hadn't popped up like a bunch of tenpins, I'd welcome the drive with the windows open and top down. Instead I have visions of tepees and a shrine. Instead of shopping center I'll have a trading post."

"Out in Utah I walked into a trading post selling straw baskets for $30,000.00. It could work here."

"Yeah, yeah, Look, I don't want to end up like Custer. Which is why you're here, Champ."

"For me to end up like Custer?"

"No, to solve this."

"Every shopping center we've done has had glitches like this."

"Assuming they let me build a shopping center."

Chipper barked their arrival. The dog strained at the end of a long rope tied to a fence post, his right eye drooping more than usual. First Mrs. and then Mr. Kruechenmeister emerged from the house.

"You just missed it, George," Mrs. Kruechenmeister said. "TV people were here and we were on Good Morning America. Come on in. Maybe they'll show it again."

"Hell," Mr. Kruechenmeister said. "We don't need you watching television. Get down there and get rid of them."

"Now Herman. There's no need to run up your blood pressure."

"A lot of them don't even look like Indians," the farmer said. "I don't trust them. They got knives and they're trespassing."

"I'm sure Mr. Roth can figure this out. Am I right, George?"

Her question caught George giving Chipper a rub.

"We'll find out" he said, not even sure of the question. Chipper, who was straining to get closer, succeeded and rose to lick his face, dragging paws down his blue sweater. George lifted her up, rubbed her ears and cheeks between his hands and put her down. "I'll see what's going on." He turned to avoid Chipper's crotch nuzzle.

"Don't be too hard on them," Mrs. K said. "They're not bad people."

"Just get rid of them," Mr. K insisted with finality, and pulled his wife toward the house.

Keys and George walked west down the slope toward maybe fifteen men and women sitting in a circle. Inside the circle sat the bones. A low chant drifted toward him through the intermittent lapses of traffic on Old Macklevee Road. TV reporters walked amidst the motionless flock followed by camera crews searching for just the right pictures. The Native Americans looked like ordinary people, making George wonder what he had expected, war paint and loin cloths. When he approached, the camera crews smelled action, abandoned the Native Americans and rushed to interview the newcomer.

George walked past them and continued to the ring of sitting bodies where an intense aroma of incense wafted around him. "I'm with the group that found the remains," he said, ignoring the camera that followed. "What's this all about?"

A paper-thin woman with light ruddy skin, wearing blue jeans and a white T-shirt, rose and walked toward him. He observed her constant gaze and firm jaw. "We are in the midst of a prayer vigil for our ancestors and prefer not to be disturbed."

"How long will you be?"

"A short time."

"Thank you," George said. Hoping for a spirit of cooperation, he moved away from the circle.

"Sir," said one of the TV men. "Would you care to tell why you're razing this burial ground?"

"I'm not razing anything."

"Apparently these Indians, these Native Americans, are protesting your dig of their ancestral remains," a woman said, microphone thrust toward him.

George walked around the TV crews and sat on the ground a respectful twenty yards from the circle. The Native Americans were chanting.

"Wouldn't you care to make a brief comment for the nine o'clock news?" said the third reporter who had followed him.

"Our talking might disturb the prayer vigil," George said in a hushed voice, though he hoped loud enough for the Native Americans to hear and appreciate. He held a forefinger to his lips.

The words "nine o'clock" played through his mind, reminding him of plans to go to Sheila's this morning. He might not make it. Meanwhile the chanting soothed him. The Native Americans' voices conspired with his fatigue to cast him into a light sleep. A police car, siren blaring, chased a speeder on Old Macklevee. George sat up straight. He had been dreaming of the air raid siren that had awakened him last week in bed with Sheila. His watch read 8:45. What happened to that "short time?"

No way he'd quickly resolve what was going on here. Maybe by ten. More likely eleven or noon. He'd have to listen, try to satisfy their concerns without hurting Keys' development. Then he'd have to convince Mr. K, who wouldn't like whatever he came up with unless Mrs. K soothed him. He might as well kiss goodbye his and Sheila's plans for the morning.

Ten minutes passed and the prayer vigil continued. Twenty minutes. The Native Americans were oblivious to the clock. A wedge of dark clouds drifted by as did the time. Occasionally he heard Chipper's bark or a noisy truck. Again he dozed until unbelievably it was 9:45. He looked around. The Native Americans, still in a circle, were talking quietly. The TV cameras, past their deadlines, were gone.

The Native American in blue jeans and T-shirt rose and walked toward George. "Mister, we'd like to speak to you. I'm Harriette Dunn from the Institute of Native American Culture. We represent the spirit of our buried ancestors."

Still in a daze George sat for a moment looking up at the woman before climbing to his feet.

"I'm George Roth. We don't own this land yet, but while —"

"You don't own this land because we own it." A man, whiter than Harriette Dunn, approached, glaring at George.

A sheathed knife hung from his belt.

"I'm George Roth." He held out his hand.

"I don't care who you are," the man said, arms folded in front of his chest, eyes unblinking. He was in his twenties, easily thirty years younger than the woman next to him. His necktie clutched his throat.

"This must feel like your land because of the graves," George said.

"This is our land," the man said. "We want you off immediately." As he talked he stepped forward until only a foot separated them. He was at least six inches taller than George.

If George showed he was intimidated, which he was, he might as well surrender. Despite the urge to take a step back, he held his gaze, and said, "Can you tell us more about your history with the land."

"We don't care what the white man's records show. A piece of paper doesn't give you land you stole. Pack up and leave."

"Mr. Roth," Harriette Dunn said, "perhaps you'd join our circle. We wish you no harm."

Sounded like a good Indian, bad Indian approach? George joined the group, sitting with legs crossed, like story telling in first grade.

"I'd like to understand your concerns," he said, "and do what we can to respect your ancestors."

"Our people have lived in these areas for thousands of years," Harriette Dunn said. "They were born here, fell in love here, raised their children on this land and died here." Her soft voice did not conceal her emotion. Her talk of ancestors made George picture real people.

"I appreciate your history. We need to find a way to preserve your heritage when we build our shopping center."

"You appreciate nothing," No Name said. "It's not the history of our people. The hearts of our people are buried where we sit."

"George." Hazel Kruechenmeister called. She walked down the hill with a large basket as though on her way to the market. "Would you and our nice guests like some hot biscuits? You can come up to the house, or if you'd rather eat them here, I brought butter and jam."

"We don't need your food," No Name scoffed and waved her away.

"We do need her agreement though," Harriette Dunn said, "so why don't we sit together. I'd love one of your biscuits."

The Native Americans made room for Mrs. K who began passing small paper plates in each direction. Steam rose from the biscuits as they broke them open. No Name refused one and glared at Mrs. K and George, mostly at George. Mrs. K passed the basket for seconds.

George could wait no longer to call Sheila. He excused himself and walked up the hill. No answer so he left a message. "I have a crisis and might be here the rest of the day. How about meeting late this afternoon?" He found Keys in his car and told him about his progress, or rather lack of progress.

"Figure it out," Keys said.

George returned to the peace conference. As he took his seat, Mrs. K said, "We've treated these people terribly. They crave their ancestors' land because our ancestors took it from them."

Had he made a mistake leaving Mrs. K with the Native Americans? She sounded ready to give away the farm.

"Harriette and I have reached an agreement."

Uh, oh, George thought.

"You and that gentleman over there probably won't like it." She pointed toward No Name. "And I'll have to plead with Mr. Kruechenmeister."

"What have you discussed?" George couldn't hide his distress.

"Our guests here, can check on the remains every day to be sure we don't disturb them. One of you can even sleep out here if you want." She spoke to the group. "Meanwhile the rest of you will leave like Mr. Kruechenmeister wants and we'll keep looking for a solution."

Mrs. Kruechenmeister had become George's negotiator. She had finished in fifteen minutes what he had been certain would take all day. She had done an end run around the angry young Native American and made a deal with Harriette Dunn who struck him as potentially reasonable. The problem wasn't gone, but it was better to keep some balls in the air than to let them crash to the ground.

Back at the car, he explained the deal to Keys. "I'm counting on you to work it out. Let me know before you agree to anything."

Just one more challenge for George's growing to-do list. He needed to meet with the Mayor, the Arts District Neighborhood Association, owners of several theaters and a jazz club, the people who owned property he wanted to buy, find a hotel operator, and eventually meet with a banker to figure out financing. Then there would be follow-ups with all of them, and he'd need to work out a deal with Emanuel Brown. Meanwhile he had a marriage, a paramour, and even a conscience to sort out. Speaking of balls in the air, he better hold onto his own.

CHAPTER 18

The first week in May George knew he was too busy to go to Paris. How to tell Bonnie? They hadn't canceled a vacation since construction of the Mid County Center had run beyond the schedule. Bonnie lived with his long hours and evening meetings, but made clear that if he devoted so much time to making money, then they'd spend some on good vacations. Vacations became untouchable.

He found her laying out cold cuts for dinner including one that filled the kitchen with a strong aroma of garlic. Her gray business suit couldn't be a size larger than the nurse's uniforms she used to wear. "Thank goodness," she said when he raised the Paris question. "I've been worried for a week about telling you I have to cancel. Hugh Collins is putting together a group of healthcare executives to brainstorm my business plan. I was afraid they'd think I wasn't a player if I ran off to Paris before I even got started."

"Who's Hugh Collins?"

"The president of CHMO. You don't remember a thing."

"What's CHMO?"

"I told you. The City-County Health Maintenance Organization." In bed that night, unable to sleep, George struggled to understand why the president of CHMO and healthcare executives were interested in Bonnie's business. He cringed at the cliché, "a player." He couldn't picture

Bonnie in business. Shifting to his side and repositioning the pillow, he thought about how disappointed his mother would be tomorrow when he told her they weren't going to Paris. Mostly asleep, he pictured himself lying on the black walnut table, surrounded by stacks of Bonnie's business papers. Keys breaks into the house and can't find him. George panics, jumps off the table and runs, Keys chasing him. He reaches the Kruechenmeister farm where he hides with Chipper. His mother, not Keys, catches him. She waves the Paris tickets in his face. He sat up in bed with a leg cramp, feeling as anxious as the time in college he got the date wrong for a final exam and had to take the test unprepared.

A packet of "Calm," mixed with water and heated in the microwave, might help his leg. On a kitchen counter he saw Bonnie's note reminding herself to call Hugh Collins, which gave him some relief, knowing she was involved with solid business people, even if they give her a lesser role with a salary. Better for her than one more volunteer position. The Calm finished, he returned to bed and within five minutes, was asleep, dreaming he installed a food court at the top of the Eiffel Tower.

"I figured you'd cancel," Helen Roth said on the phone. "I have Sunny Middlebaum on standby so I won't forfeit the tickets."

"Isn't Sunny's wife ill?"

"She died three years ago, George."

"Mom, I don't see how you can handle a trip to Paris."

"You're upset I'm going with a man. You're afraid we'll have sex?"

"Have all the sex you want. Do you need to go to Paris to have it?"

"Unfortunately, sex with Sunny is wishful thinking. However, we will be on that plane."

And she was. On the last day of April, George drove her to the airport, where she refused a wheelchair. "Got to keep fit for Paris."

"You can take cabs," George said.

"But the subway is where you get pinched on the ass." They met Sunny Middlebaum and his daughter at security. Bent slightly at the waist, Sunny looked like he'd need more help than his mother.

"Why don't you use the Porsche while I'm away," she offered as she thrust her prostheses and herself into line. "You ought to have a little fun while I'm having dinner at Maxim's."

As he drove the Porsche to his office, George wondered if Maxim's still existed and whether it was still a famous restaurant. Pushing and pulling the Porsche's controls reminded him of being a kid playing pinball at the corner drug store. The Porsche gave him a sense of freedom like when he was sixteen and got his license.

At the office Harriette Dunn, No Name, and George called the Bureau of Indian Affairs and then concluded that the remains were from a prehistoric tribe of the fourteenth or fifteenth century. The Osage might have been in the area during the early 1800s but they had buried their dead in mounds above ground.

"Any suggestions for what we do?" Harriette said.

"The only acceptable suggestion is to deed us the land," No Name said in a measured voice, unlike back at the farm.

"We could deed you a small piece of the farm, not where the bones are now, which likely is not where your ancestors lived."

"We're entitled to the entire farm and much more."

George knew the Native Americans had no legal right under existing laws and also knew to confront No Name with this would likely extend the conflict. Instead he said, "I know our settlors took land that wasn't theirs, maybe this land, maybe not. Over years attitudes have changed. We'd like to meet everyone's expectations."

"What are your thoughts?" Harriette said.

"Here's one, fairly simple." Keys had already approved it. "We would carefully excavate all the remains and move them to a place near the road where we would build a monument, available to visitors."

"They can't be displayed and need to be reburied."

"Okay. We or you will rebury them and then you can prepare an exhibit to educate people, including if you want, how westward expansion displaced your ancestors. It will become a cultural site."

"We'd want full control of the exhibit," No Name said.

"As long as it's accurate. And located separate from the shopping center."

"Why's that?" No Name said.

"It should be clear that it's your organization's exhibit."

George wondered about Mr. Kreuchenmeister's reaction to having a Native-American shrine near St. Isidore's. The two together could teach religious and cultural tolerance, but now was not the time to raise that possibility. The Kreuchenmeisters had already bought a house in Florida. Soon Keys would own the farm. Hopefully the problem was solved and he could work fulltime on his own project and have time with Sheila.

CHAPTER 19

In May Sheila told her Kansas City client she needed "think" time, two weeks at home. George dropped by every day, twice one day. They were like teenagers discovering sex when their parents were out of town. Though they spent most of their time in bed, Sheila's wackiness appealed to him as much as her body. One day, while she lay on her back with his head resting near her breast and his hand exploring her tummy, he asked whether she preferred a horizontal caress to a vertical caress. She sat up, letting his head bounce on the mattress. "George, you sound like my eye doctor: is it better with lens A or lens B?"

"I love how you say whatever comes to your mind," he said.

"I should teach you."

"Please."

"I'd like to know more about you. You know about my daughter, my ex-marriage, the custody battle, how I love the variety of my job."

And so began a change in their relationship. Leisurely he told stories about his children, ambivalence about Harry Keys, the importance of his job.

"Is your job an escape from something?" she asked. George said he had the same question. He spent time in the car, in bed before falling to sleep, even at the office wondering whether his job was an escape and if so, from what? Sheila was changing his life, making him more aware of what was going on in his life and why.

Meanwhile, he had never been busier. Both Sheila and he were making followup calls to solicitors to keep them focused on completing their fundraising calls. He had several meetings at the Family Planning Center for input on new levels of security. He met with Binta and Emanuel Brown to identify which properties to pursue, and generally to define what to put where. How many residential units, whether they should be high rise or townhouses, what retail to mix with the residential, whether office space should be above retail or on separate land. Work plus time with Sheila made for long days.

If he had paid more attention, he would have realized what Bonnie was up to a lot sooner. He might have asked the telling questions the morning the man carried the Xerox machine into the kitchen. But it was a small table top model and even though he was certain Bonnie could just as easily have gone to the FedEx store for copies, he didn't say anything. Besides he could use it too. And then there were endless meetings with nurses, physical therapists, phlebotomists. How many could she be hiring? He figured a few but that meetings continued because they kept turning her down.

Perhaps he was so involved in the Arts District and with Sheila that he wouldn't have noticed if Bonnie had been on the cover of Fortune Magazine. No matter how busy he was he should have seen that Bonnie had changed. Perhaps he had known all along and unconsciously rooted her on, as though a business for Bonnie justified Sheila for him. Maybe he didn't want to notice his wife's achievements. Or worse, at least in George's eyes, he paid so little attention, that he might not have noticed regardless what she did.

He couldn't help but take heed one Thursday in May when Stan Arnold, his lawyer, called. After the usual chit-chat, Arnold asked, "Will you be there so I can messenger over the lease?"

"What lease?" What on earth was Arnold talking about?

"The office lease. You need to co-sign."

"We own our building. You helped us buy it."

"Bonnie's office, George. I'm sending the lease for Bonnie's business."

"Stan, I'm not aware of Bonnie's lease, nor was I aware she had hired you as her attorney." His lawyer's five-hundred-dollar hourly rate made him cringe.

"You're kidding," Arnold said. "It's no secret." He proceeded to tell George he had formed an LLC for Bonnie. She was leasing office space in the Central West End, not far from many of the hospitals and the CHMO building as well as the Arts District. After Memorial Day, 33 nurses, 8 nurse-practitioners, 2 physical therapists, a phlebotomist, one telephone dispatcher and two people to handle insurance and Medicare paper work were going on his wife's payroll. She already had contracts with enough hospitals, HMOs and insurance companies to pretty much insure a profit.

"The big item," Arnold said, "is not so much this lease but her revolving loan from River National Bank you have to sign. It firmed up only last week, but I'm amazed you didn't know. Half a million right off the bat plus a five million standby for future growth. It's the largest revolver they've ever done with a startup. This is going to be really big." George heard more excitement in Arnold's voice than the lawyer had ever shown for any of his shopping centers. Did the damn lawyer picture Bonnie as a bigger client?

"Where's Bonnie now, Stan?"

"She called ten minutes ago. I don't know where she went, but why don't you try her mobile?"

George was too embarrassed to admit he didn't know her mobile number so he told Dalton to deliver the lease to his house and drove home to wait. What could she possibly be doing? Thirty-three nurses at … they must make twenty-five dollars an hour, that's a thousand a week, fifty-two thousand a year, times thirty-three. He scratched it out, over a million seven a year for just the nurses. The decimal has got to be in the wrong place. And that doesn't even count those nurse practicers or whatever they were called.

George tried to work on his own papers while he waited for Bonnie. He sat at the black walnut table staring at the pages which might as well have been written in Arabic. All he could think about were Bonnie's risky commitments. His wife had no business experience. She was committing them to pay back millions of dollars. She didn't know how to manage people. She'd lose control. She'd lose his money. At two forty-five the garage door rumbled open.

"George," she exclaimed. "What are you doing here?"

"Stan called about this." He held up the lease. "Don't you think I ought to know something about your business before I start signing papers?" He couldn't hide irritation from Bonnie like he could from bankers and tenants. If she didn't explode now, she would soon.

"I should have called you myself, Honey," she said. "By the time Stan called about the lease, I was late for a meeting with Hugh Collins, so I ran. I apologize."

"Hugh Collins? I know you've told me who he is."

"The head of CHMO. A delightful man. You'll enjoy meeting him."

"Bonnie, you're thousands of dollars down the road in commitments I don't know a thing about. Why didn't you tell me?"

"You're so busy with your project and Binta Brown. I didn't want to bother you until I had to."

"When you're asking me to sign, don't you think I should know?"

"I've been so careful like you've been all these years with our commitments for your shopping centers. You've always protected us. Hugh Collins and others looked at my business plan and suggested I hire Deloite Touche to go over it. They're all positive and enthusiastic."

George started and then abandoned the math on what Deloite Touche might cost. "I'd like to get my two cents in before you go ahead."

"That's wonderful, George. Both your mother and Helen Cohen thought you wouldn't be interested. If you are, I'd love to have you take a look. You have to be quick though because of the fantastic news I just heard from Hugh."

"What's that?"

"In six weeks the CHMO Board of Directors is giving me a kickoff dinner at the Hunt Club. You and all the other spouses are invited."

For a moment George felt dizzy. He had never been to the Hunt Club, with its plantation-like mansion, French chef and golf course, all for the 25 or so CEOs of the city's major companies, who were the club's only members. All at once he began to laugh, loud, with Sheila-like mirth.

"What's so funny," Bonnie laughed back, and for the first time since she arrived home, George realized she hadn't blown up. She was handling him.

"I'm laughing because I never thought I'd be invited to the Hunt Club, and now you're taking me."

"Aren't you excited," Bonnie said though she ought to know damn well he'd be just the opposite. "You need to try on your tux."

CHAPTER 20

George was bothered by more than his tight tuxedo. Bonnie had created a whole new life and he had hardly noticed. Partly because of Sheila. Even without Sheila, Bonnie's and his lives had become automatic with little connection. They saw friends, went to restaurants and movies, sometimes watched television. But what did they appreciate and consider special? No TV program they delighted watching every week. No books they read and discussed. They no longer had their children's issues to consider now that both lived out of town and were thriving. Sadly, he didn't feel compelled to make more of an effort, initiate an activity, expand their sexual routine.

To George's dismay Sheila's answering service took his call. She had left for Kansas City. Wouldn't be back until Friday. He didn't leave a message. When she returned, they had a quickie over the weekend when Bonnie had a meeting, satisfying but not fulfilling. No romance. How had their relationship become routine so quickly? Maybe a quickie was a sign for their relationship either to end or to expand. When Sheila told him that she would be out of town for much of the coming month, he was half disappointed and half relieved.

Sheila's week-long absences became a blessing. He and Binta accomplished some pre-development tasks. The city welcomed the project though they foisted road and sidewalk improvements onto them if they went ahead. He called Molly Ponce at the Catholic Legal Ministry at the Archdiocese and asked if she could arrange for Binta to meet with the Archbishop or others at the Archdiocese who might want to hear about the development. He suggested Binta out of concern that the Archbishop might equate him with the Family Planning Center abortion service. Binta discovered a group that built and operated "play-knowledge museums" that had experiences for both children and their parents, a great draw of people, which would enhance the entire area.

Sheila's absence gave time and distance to consider their relationship, which he admitted was more than sex. Her playfulness was infectious, making him aware that play wasn't one of Bonnie's qualities. Bonnie was steady. How Sheila's whimsy fit with her successful business career puzzled him. Consultants provided analysis, logic and presentations rather than playful spontaneity. His analysis didn't do justice to how his heart felt about Bonnie and Sheila. Being drawn to both of them confused and frustrated him. A momentary fantasy, running off with Binta, seemed like relief from being torn between his wife and mistress.

He decided to end the relationship. When Sheila called and invited him to come over Friday afternoon after she got back to town, George lied: "I have a late meeting." He suggested Saturday morning at the Botanical Garden, which opened at seven.

"Tell me which bush I'll find you behind," Sheila said.

⇋

George grabbed his mother's bags from the carousel that circled like a roulette wheel in slow motion. Helen Roth blew a kiss to Sunny Middlebaum who shuffled off to the garage with his daughter. Bonnie had just gone for the SAAB so George walked slowly with his mother while travelers scurried around them.

"I picked up a fabulous idea for a new business I'm going to start," she said.

"You too?"

"Wait till we're in the car so Bonnie can hear. Just as good you didn't go to Paris. Too much fun for you."

"You had a good time," he ignored her tease. Her caustic humor brought him a sense of relief. She was okay. Her body had held up.

"All except for the Ritz. Too fancy, so we found a place on the Left Bank."

He put his mother in the front seat and sat in the back. Better to have her tell Bonnie how to drive.

As they wove through the spaghetti of exit ramps and feeder lanes into the highway system, Helen Roth related tidbits of Paris. "Maxim's is nothing compared to our favorite on Rue Jacob. The owner keeps a sofa in the street in front of the place where he drinks schnapps with his friends. Sunny and I are welcome any time."

She didn't mention her "fabulous idea for a new business." George hoped she'd forget. But as soon as she and Bonnie finished unpacking, she said, "Now I'll tell you how I'm going to get rich. Every morning we had a fantastic breakfast. One day it just came to me. We need a croissant shop in town. It's obvious. I'll sell croissants and other rolls in the morning and sweets in the afternoon and evening."

"It could work," Bonnie said.

"I'm ready to start. Just like you're starting your business."

"That's wonderful," Bonnie said. "If I weren't into my thing I'd do it with you."

"I even have a name: 'Crazy Croissants.'"

"Just a minute." George tried to slow her down. "How will you do this?"

"One croissant at a time. At one of your shopping centers. West County types will eat up this French stuff."

Crazy Croissants perfectly described the idea. His seventy-seven-year-old mother starting a business was the zaniest thing George had ever heard. He couldn't imagine her baking croissants at four in the morning and closing up at night. Little shops couldn't afford a lot of extra help. He knew not to challenge her, for if he did, they'd argue for an hour and it was already two A.M. Paris time. "We'll talk about it," he said, "but for now let's get some sleep."

"George, it would be perfect for her," Bonnie said in the car.

"She can't handle a store."

"A typical male response. If she were your father instead of your mother you'd think it was terrific."

"Not for a seventy-seven-year-old legless father."

"Use your imagination. All you have to do is find her a partner to do the leg work. Running a store sure beats her driving that car."

Worrying about croissants kept George's mind off Sheila most of Friday. His mother called early to say she was putting together a "business plan," which Sunny had told her was necessary to obtain a loan. Bonnie, who thought it easy for his mother to find a partner, of course was out for the day.

Friday night George forgot croissants. He lay in bed thinking how in the morning he would tell Sheila it was over. Relief from guilt and anxiety at last. At three A.M., certain he wouldn't sleep, he threw on his sweats and walked around the Arts District. In a few hours he'd meet Sheila and reclaim his soul. He would put his life back on the automatic pilot of habit, work and family.

When he returned to bed, he dreamt that he was in a washing machine, rocking back and forth, cleansed.

At the Garden, he waited for Sheila, listening to the reedy call of a red-winged blackbird amidst the floral aromas set against the sound of water falling from a fountain. Waves of dancing tulips would attract thousands today, but at seven A.M., George and two workers had the garden to themselves. It was not the kind of setting in which he would expect to panic.

"How's my sex object?" came Sheila's lyrical voice behind him. Her laughter drowned out the fountain. "I've always wanted to get laid here," she said in not quite a whisper.

"Shh." George was unable to force back a smile as he looked around to see if they were alone. Relax, he told himself.

"No one's here, scaredy. I looked," Sheila said.

"Let's walk." George steered her toward a path.

Sheila refused to be guided. First she stopped to examine ants crawling all over the blooming peonies. "If we all worked this hard, we'd never have any fun," she said.

"Let's talk while we walk," George said, but Sheila darted ahead to where she mimicked the contorted pose of a statue named the "Grand Baigneuse."

"I love these names." She danced along what looked like an overgrown weed garden. "Catmint... , Veronica... , Ceratostigma... . Taste this sage." She tore a leaf from a plant and crumbled it between her thumb and forefinger. The smell was okay but when Sheila tried to push it into his mouth, he blew it away.

"Sheila, calm down," he scolded, but she forged ahead. "Angel's Hair, Speedwell, Life Forever, Lambs-Ears. Isn't that a great name, Lambs-Ears?"

Only Picasso would have thought the plant looked like a lamb's ear.

"Toadflax is more how I feel," he said.

Sheila settled beside him and slipped her arm through his, which made him uncomfortable. "We need to talk," he said.

"We need to find a place to make love so you feel better. Right here in the Hosta Garden would be perfect. With this breeze, we could thrash around for hours and everyone would think it was the wind."

She tugged his arm and edged them toward the thick foliage. Using his hip to block her like a basketball player, he returned her to the path. She turned in front of him, pulled him toward her and locked him into a kiss. No one George had made out with could kiss like Sheila. When he pulled away, he had to give his pants a little jiggle.

"George, I know you're trying to dump me. That's not what you really want, and before I give you up, you have to convince me I'm wrong."

"Sheila, I can't handle this. Call me square, a lousy liar, anything you want, but I'm not made for it."

"Did you ever notice all the flaws in this garden?" she said.

Now what? "We're talking about us."

"I defy you to find a weed in this garden. No garden is real without weeds."

"What about us, Sheila?"

"And look at all those daylily signs." She pointed ahead where someone had stuck easily a hundred foot-high signs in rows as straight as a battalion of marines.

"What about them?"

"The problem," Sheila said, "is that in another month little plants are going to come out of the ground and obscure those beautiful signs they went to so much trouble to plant."

"Sheila, be serious. We need to go back to fund raising."

"Why, because you're married? I haven't heard you say you love your wife. Forget the shoulds and shouldn'ts. Decide what you want."

A hundred times he had run it through his mind. An affair wouldn't work. When he met Bonnie twenty-three years ago, he had been sleeping with another woman every weekend. He liked Bonnie right away and told the other woman they had to stop seeing each other. She didn't understand why they couldn't go to bed once a week, on Wednesday or Thursday if he wanted, at least until Bonnie and he got married. He couldn't do that. It made no sense to him, just like Sheila was making no sense. He was trying to have a logical discussion about adultery, and she wanted to poke fun at the garden and fuck in the Hosta.

They started down the hill into the Japanese Garden, a mistake because halfway around, Sheila tried to hustle him across the forbidden bridge to the temple that was closed to the public. He had always wanted to go across the bridge. One night at a jazz concert in the Garden Amphitheater, Bonnie drank too much wine and tried to pull him out there–it was dark enough they could have made it–but he dragged her away.

"Sheila, we're not going there. It's protected by oriental

poison."

"Oriental love potion more likely. But you're right, we can be more creative."

"Let's get some coffee." He steered them back toward the main building, where they served breakfast. The presence of other people would keep Sheila in line. And keep him in line.

"We're coming to the worst flaw of all in this supposedly world-class garden."

"What's that?" Better to play her mind game than her body game.

"They've spelled 'Climatron' wrong," she said referring to the three-story geodesic dome that looked like giant glass-covered tinker-toys.

"I don't think so," he said as they got close enough to read the sign.

"They left out the 'b'. If they're going to use a fancy name for a 'Jungle Gym,' they should at least spell it, C-l-i-m-b-a-t-r-o-n."

Even George laughed. They were within sight of the safe-haven restaurant. "Sheila, you're great fun, but you're right. I want to end our affair."

That was the instant he panicked. He panicked because he saw twenty-five or thirty members from Temple Isaiah. He didn't have to panic. He could have walked right up to the group and introduced Sheila like they had harmlessly run into each other or like they had picked the garden for their fundraising planning. Instead, when he saw Isabel

Fischer who could spread a rumor faster than the flu, he grabbed Sheila's arm and dragged her down the main walk past the reflecting ponds. She ran with him, probably thinking he had suddenly changed his mind about making love. Up ahead lay a small thick plot of bamboo trees. He headed for them and pulled Sheila through the tightly spaced pole-like trunks, which were so thin and close together he was afraid they'd break. But they didn't. Ten yards deep was like being miles away in a forest. As they moved ahead there was a small open spot, wide enough to stand very close together, trees all around them. He looked back and couldn't see out.

CHAPTER 21

"How daring, sweetheart," Sheila said, but he put his hand over her mouth.

"There are thirty people from my temple coming this way," he whispered. "Stand still and don't talk."

They heard the voices and shuffling feet. George held his breath, afraid Sheila would do something crazy. She hugged him tight. Their breathing sounded like the roar of a giant panda he imagined eating its way toward them.

"Let's stop here," came Rabbi Isaacs' voice. "This is just fine for our service."

Then George remembered. Today the Temple was conducting its Sabbath service at the Garden in recognition of Arbor Day. A month ago George had called the Garden's director to obtain permission to drink tiny thimbles of wine. Somehow he had forgotten the occasion, probably because Bonnie and he went to temple only for High Holidays. He had arranged his rendezvous with Sheila in the lap of thirty people he knew.

If the group wasn't right next to the bamboo patch, they couldn't be ten feet away. He stifled a laugh at the image of him and Sheila walking out, pretending they had arrived for the service. Maybe he could sneak out and walk up behind the members as though he had come late. Then Sheila could duck out and take off. He questioned whether he could whisper this strategy without being overheard. Would Sheila even cooperate?

"BORUCH ATTOH ADONOY ELOHAYNU MELECH HO'OLOM ASHER KIDD'SHONU B'MITZVOSOV V'TZIVONU L'HADLIK NER SHEL SHABBAT." Rabbi Isaacs' words floated through on the wind. "We thank You, Lord our God, Creator of the universe, …"

At that point Sheila unzipped his fly. Slowly she threaded her hand through the slot in his boxer shorts. Her fingers moved back and forth, almost imperceptibly. He couldn't maneuver away without shaking the trees and exposing their presence. One of the congregants might pick herself through the bamboo to see what was going on.

"Sheila," he whispered.

"Shh. Don't let the people hear."

As he grew, he pressed his hand into the narrow space between them and tried to remove her hand. She resisted. The bamboo trees around them shook. He froze and Sheila's hand moved faster.

"Sheila…" Before he could say more, he no longer wanted her to stop. He began caressing the back of her neck, and with his other hand pulled up her skirt. Then he worked his hand down the back of her panties and around to the damp front.

"BORUCH ATTOH ADONOY ELOHAYNU MELECH HO'OLOM BORAY P'REE HAGOFEN." The words interrupted George's passion long enough to conclude he had gone crazy. Or rather had been crazy for some time.

Before he could process this thought, Sheila had coupled them. He couldn't "just say no," even though he knew they'd soon be thrashing so hard they'd give themselves away. But he was wrong. Without moving her body, Sheila began squeezing and releasing, over and over, something she later told him was her pubococcygeus muscle, a muscle that if properly trained, she proclaimed, would allow a woman to rearrange two Ping Pong balls within her vagina. He struggled to be silent. George cared about nothing but Sheila.

The congregation stayed until nine. Some said goodbye while others spoke of walking around the Garden. At nine-fifteen he pushed out the side and prayed that Sheila would keep her word and wait ten minutes.

He ran into Rabbi Isaacs in the parking lot. "We missed you in the Garden," the Rabbi said.

"I had a meeting I couldn't cancel. We met here so I could join you if I finished in time."

George didn't interrupt as the Rabbi described the Arbor Day service and then said, "Your name is at the top of my list to organize the children's carnival at the Temple."

Just what I need, George thought. "Why not one of the fathers who still has a child in the Sunday School?"

"Their turns will come, but I ask all the members eventually. I'm sure you can handle it."

So it seemed as he decided it wasn't worth more discussion.

⇋

Binta took classes during the summer so she would have her MBA in December. Still she had time to put together a list of retail uses they should consider for the project. XLPOR stood at the top of her list. The company provided hands-on, science and technology exhibits as well as broader activities like interactive construction, art, and cooking.

Together George and Binta called XLPOR and reached Billie Johnson, their new-location rep. Billie said she would be in the Midwest in August.

"Too late," George said. "Where will you be next week?"

"Meetings in New York."

"We'll come to you."

"That's not necessary, Mr. Roth, and I have to be honest. I'm working on Denver and Phoenix for our next locations."

"Call me George, please. I like to travel in the spring. We could fly in for dinner, give you an idea of what we have and not interfere with your schedule."

"You're certainly accommodating, George."

They agreed to meet in Billie's office in a little more than a week.

George and Binta spent several days putting together a proposal for Billie. Which prompted a phone call from Sheila.

"Why are you hiding from me?" she said with a laugh. Sheila could laugh while she talked. George had tried it alone in the car but sounded ridiculous. "Do we need to break up again at the Botanical Garden?"

George explained what he and Binta were doing. "One of these days the two of you will meet. I'm sure you'll like each other."

"Just teasing. I've probably got more conflicts than you. I'm gone until Saturday."

George forgot his "no weekends" pledge. He penciled "drive trade area" into his day planner for Saturday morning, an innocuous note if Bonnie happened to see it.

The bumpy flight to New York in a full airplane and indifferent service reminded him why he hated to fly. Airplanes made him think of retirement. But retirement brought forth a vision of walking around the park with a metal detector looking for coins. He imagined Bonnie a success, coming home at the end of the day and praising him for finding seventy-five cents. He sighed, closed his eyes and thanked God he had his mixed-use development.

The next morning, warm and sunny, they walked 20 blocks to XLPOR. A New York rush hour provided throngs of people hustling on the streets and darting in and out of little shops that radiated bakery and coffee aromas.

Surprise: not that XLPOR's receptionist was a man, which he was, but that he resembled Thomas Edison in a turn-of-the century suit with two different wigs available so that he could be either a young or older Edison.

"When does Alice Ball take over?" Binta asked Edison.

"Alice Ball?"

"An African American woman who developed the first treatment for leprosy."

"Wonderful," Edison said. "I'm due to move on from this job and she'd make the perfect successor."

Billie must have said to send them back because Edison pointed to a door. The second it closed behind them, the lights went out. Total darkness. George tried to reopen it, but it was locked. Slowly rows of lanterns on the walls dimly lit an empty corridor that was as long as the building. It felt like a spook house where any minute a skeleton would drop or Dracula would appear. Two right turns were the only options at the far end and led them back toward where they had started. They never made it. After a dozen steps, a door slid closed behind them. Then another ahead of them. They stood in a five-by-five cubicle. Again, the lights went off. George groped along the walls, imagining sets of eyes peering through tiny holes. Then the wall to his left opened.

A woman beckoned. She didn't resemble any scientist George could recall.

"How do you like our office, Mr. Roth? I mean George." She held out her hand. "I'm Billie."

George introduced Binta who said, "I like it a lot. Nothing like mind-numbing business school."

"Exactly. I doubt that you've had courses in creativity. The boss, we call him the Wizard, designed the entry into our space so that it separates us and our visitors from the everyday world into a world of creativity." She handed them an XLPOR annual statement. "We make lots of money because the Wizard keeps our business-school people in another location. Have a seat."

Billie moved some Lego structures to the side of her desk. "It's a new form of Monopoly based on shopping center properties — XLPOR employees are encouraged to develop new exhibits."

"Prepare to advance token to the Grand Odyssey" George said. "Binta's name for our project. You're going to love this location." He walked her through the executive summary of their brochure that emphasized proximity and incomes of residents and tourists plus the other attractions in the Arts District.

"What do you think?" he asked. She took a pencil and after several false starts moved XPOLR to a prominent place. "We could do that," he said.

"A project with potential," Billie said.

"Shall we send a lease?" Binta said.

"Not so fast."

"Okay. I'll use the mail rather than Fed Ex."

Billie answered Binta's smile with a laugh. "I like your spirit," she said. "First I'll show you the kinds of exhibits and activities we develop."

They walked through more sparsely lit corridors and through doors that opened as they approached, leading to a long corridor with padded walls. A unicycle leaned against one wall next to a small basket with 3 balls. "This is our Claude and Mary Shannon Exhibit," Billie said. "We teach visitors to juggle the 3 balls, then to ride the unicycle and then do both at the same time. Claude Shannon discovered what became computer logic when he was still in graduate school. Mary worked with Claude at Bell Labs where together they discovered and developed information theory. Claude used to do his best thinking while he rode his unicycle back and forth in the long Bell-Labs corridors while juggling the balls."

"He must have a Nobel Prize," George said.

"They don't give a Nobel for mathematics," Billie said. "He won the Kyoto Prize, Japan's equivalent to the Nobel for mathematics."

While Binta successfully rode the unicycle, George restrained himself from drooling over the prospect of locating XLPOR in the Grand Odyssey. The padded walls saved his life on both of his unicycle attempts, though he successfully juggled the balls while standing on both feet and then one foot.

Billie and Binta applauded and then Billie escorted them into the Ada Lovelace room. There the exhibit showed what the Shannons had discovered. And then it explained how in 1843 Ada Lovelace wrote about how computers can go beyond number-crunching and perform other functions, exemplified by the Shannons' work.

"Many people don't want to try the unicycle, so we lead them into this room."

Over the next hour Billie took them through a kitchen where visitors helped prepare a Michelin 3-star-restaurant meal, a virtual batting cage where they tried to connect with a Sandy Koufax fastball, and an exercise class where visitors watched a movie of an autopsy that exposed muscle groups as the class exercised to strengthen those groups.

Back in Billie's office, George said, "How about you and the Wizard coming to take a look at what we offer?" Billie agreed to come without the Wizard. "He won't give up going to Denver but maybe down the road." Driving to the airport George was ecstatic. "Billie was half sold. We're a long way from groundbreaking but we need to come up with an excuse to have a ground-breaking kind of event when she comes."

CHAPTER 22

George and Binta secured options on six parcels in the Grand Avenue area, none as difficult to negotiate as it had been with the Kruechenmeisters. They worked together as a team. Binta with her congenial, open personality easily established rapport with both Black and white owners. George provided the business experience and important terms, which Binta quickly learned. She aligned herself with the sellers by making light fun of George's driven, analytic manner. "Can't we slow down, George," she would say. "We'll never get in bed together without a little romance."

"Where did you learn that one," he asked after they left the meeting.

"I made it up with my first boyfriend," Binta said.

A seventh owner was holding out for too much money. They could build without his land, but the project would be significantly better with it.

The option prices and construction-cost information obtained from Emanuel Brown gave enough information to develop a rough budget. They submitted the budget to River National Bank with a request for the bank to consider a development loan of $100 million dollars.

Hank Smoltz greeted Binta and George in the reception area on the Bank's twelfth floor. The assistant vice president, who usually met George in shirtsleeves, was wearing a black suit. He carried three stuffed accordion files, the kind that don't tie shut, forcing Hank to push here and there with his free hand to keep the papers from falling.

"That's okay," George said, signaling Hank not to shift the files to shake hands. "What are these."

"Files for all your loans," Smoltz said. "We're meeting Mr. Smith upstairs." Smoltz pushed a button for an elevator across the hall.

"This deal stands alone," George said. "Ms. Brown and her family are doing this project with me. Harry Keys isn't involved."

"I think Mr. Smith knows that but he asked me to bring the files." Smoltz stood at the back of the elevator and avoided George's eyes.

The elevator didn't seem to move, yet the door opened to peach-colored carpet on the thirty-fifth floor. Ahead lay a wide corridor with offices so far apart they reminded George of mansions in a gated community. Secretaries sat at neat desks beyond the reception area doing administrative tasks, no typing or fondling reams of computer paper.

Spencer Elliot Smith, the senior vice-president who handled Keys and George's loans at River National Bank, sat hunched over a file at a glass table in the middle of his office. With long legs and a slight body, he looked like a twice-bent swizzle stick stuffed into a Manhattan glass.

Smith's regular appearance on the newspaper's society page always portrayed more gadabout than banker. Recent clippings hadn't captured that both his hair and his thin, clipped mustache had turned gray. Hollywood could cast him in a tuxedo at some state department function.

Smith half rose and beckoned for Binta and George to take a seat, making George wonder if preferred customers received a full stand-up.

"Spencer," George said and held out his hand to the banker whose cologne smelled like a mixture of coconut and almond, as though he had come to a costume party as a pina colada. "Meet Binta Brown, my partner on this Arts District Project."

"Good of you to come down to the Bank, Binta and Mr. Roth, it's Sam isn't it?"

George corrected him. Smith said "The Bank" like the anchor on the evening news said, "The White House."

"I'm sorry. I went to college with a Sam Roth. Let me put these papers aside. I'm working with the Bank examiners who are crawling all over our loan portfolio."

"Don't let those guys get you down, Spencer. All they see is real estate nuclear winter."

Just then the door swung open and in walked Walter Blake, chairman of the board.

"Hey Spence," he said.

"Walter, say hello to George Roth and Binta Brown who are here to discuss a loan for a mixed-use project in the Arts District. George, do you know Walter Blake?" he said giving the name the prominence a news anchor would give the president.

"Hi Walter." They had met somewhere that George couldn't remember. Like everyone in town, he knew about Blake, voted by Fortune or Business Week or some magazine as one of the ten best bankers in the country. Anyone who envisioned a project like a new stadium or "save the schools program" sought Blake's support first. At one time he had been Chairman of the Republican National Committee, maybe still was.

"George, nice to see you. And Ms. Brown, are you related to Emanuel?"

"My father."

"Give Manny my regards. George, I was about to ask Spence to contribute to Ellie Martin's primary campaign. Can we add you to the list?"

"Walter, I'm supporting Martha Hill." George referred to the pro-choice City Council candidate who had come forward to counter Ellie Martin's right to life position. He made a mental note to ask the bank for money for the Family Planning Center.

"I'm supporting Martin," Binta said. "I'll be glad to make a contribution."

"Wonderful, and George, how about the Symphony?" Blake said. "This is solicitation day. I don't let anyone off the thirty-fifth floor without drawing blood."

Blake's arm twisting was legendary. In one story, he had tampered with the security system that locked the bank's doors after hours. A conference room full of business types, investment bankers, lawyers, all working late on what looked like a doomed merger, couldn't leave and by morning Blake had wrung out an agreement.

"The Symphony's one of my favorites," George said. "If Spencer here doesn't break my back with a high interest rate, I'd be delighted to increase the amount Bonnie already contributed."

"Spence, what are you doing to this poor man?"

"Mr. Roth and the Browns have an interesting project. I'm a little worried that George is in trouble with that anti-abortion group. They might cause him trouble."

"Oh yes," Blake said. "Roth, stay away from abortion. Nothing but trouble."

George pictured a red herring. Smith and Blake might talk abortion, but had probably discussed their real hang-up, that the project was located in the city, not far from the north side where the establishment kept pushing African Americans. Now that Blacks outnumbered whites in the City, Black politicians didn't seem to fight the segregation as much, since they had the votes to control city government, assuming they arranged wards strategically.

"I'm sure you can work it out," Blake said as he departed.

Smith said he'd be glad to recommend the loan if George pledged his interests in his other shopping centers. George explained that he had an agreement with Keys that neither of them could borrow against their interests without the consent of the other.

"After you called to discuss this," Smith said, "I had a conversation with Keys that he would consent to your pledging your interests because you've given each other the right to buy out the other if this loan goes bad."

The Keys connection smacked George like one of Keys' barbells. Keys was probably betting against the Grand Odyssey. "Have you given Keys a commitment to finance his purchase of my interests."

"Unofficially, and we give you the same if you buy him out. This all assumes your other centers are doing well at the time."

Like it or not, the banks controlled most deals. He took the risks, put in the effort, and if he made the right decisions and had some luck, he came out well, sometimes very well. Still the banks always made a profit as long as they didn't take crazy risks like they had back before 2008.

Smith agreed to send him a loan commitment that George knew would have so many conditions that it didn't commit to anything that the bank didn't want to do at the time of the loan. Which was okay. If the bank didn't want the deal, he probably wouldn't either. For planning purposes, he knew what it would take to obtain a loan.

CHAPTER 23

With his Native American problem solved, Keys completed the purchase of the Kreuchenmeister farm. The contract required Keys to take custody of Chipper, and when he said he was going to put Chipper down, George objected and took Chipper home.

Bonnie questioned how they could look after a dog with their modest-sized lot and back yard. "You probably expect me to feed and walk him," she said. "I just don't have the time these days."

"I think he likes me," George said. "I'll make it work." He built a fence so Chipper could be outside, plus a lean-to with a doggie door to the house. Most days he made time to come home and take Chipper for a neighborhood walk or on some days, a romp in a park. On days he travelled, a twelve-year-old neighborhood entrepreneur filled in for a fee.

It was love at first sight when he took Chipper to Sheila's. They wrestled on the grass and made dog-like noises in harmony. George wondered what Chipper thought when she lay on the floor at the foot of Sheila's bed while Sheila and he made love. Could this be bad dog-parenting?

"Don't worry," Sheila said. "Take him to a dog shrink if he gets confused. But pray he doesn't learn to talk."

George's apprehension over Bonnie's evening at the Hunt Club grew as he fumbled with the shirt studs he hadn't inserted since his roommate's marriage two years after college. The front of his pants came within an inch of buttoning. Not bad. He pinned the cummerbund to his shirt to be sure it didn't slip.

Before signing onto Bonnie's loan, he read her business plan. Deloitte Touche, River National Bank and even his own lawyer all thought she would be a success. What was he going to do? Veto all of them and make a fool of his wife? She probably hadn't planned it, but she had boxed him in as cleverly as Keys had ever manipulated anyone. His own neglect also contributed to his lack of options for input about her plans.

What was the source of his apprehension about tonight's event? At times in his life George had bristled over being excluded from activities and places because he was Jewish. It frustrated him because there was nothing he could do about it. He was Jewish, happy to be Jewish, and wouldn't trade his Jewish identity for acceptance. Still being excluded gave him an image of treading water next to the Titanic because there wasn't enough room in the life boat.

The Hunt Club was different. He would be a member regardless of his religion if he ran a big company, a position he considered out of reach. Even if he had taken a different route in life and gone to work for a large corporation, he couldn't picture himself leading a huge organization. Hunt

Club members headed work forces of thousands, approved budgets of billions, hired people who figured out what the boss wanted without asking. CHMO's prestigious board included three Hunt Club members. Ironically George's performance in his business affected his financial well-being much more directly than those three who drew down their twenty-million-dollar salaries even when their companies lost money.

It wasn't that he was jealous, George thought as he redid the bow tie. Maybe twenty years ago he would have been jealous, before his own success.

Regardless of how George felt about the Hunt Club, he would never have guessed how well Bonnie would play. She circulated triumphantly in a gown he'd never seen, with its thin straps and moderately loose front that passed as tasteful while attracting glances. Like from the electric-products company maven now talking with her and Hugh Collins, who had his arm across her back and hand on her shoulder. Bonnie was talking and then the three of them laughed, probably over a story George had brushed away. A white-coated waiter passed hors d'oeuvres, and George chose a frail looking piece of toast covered with a thin spread of cream cheese and a thimble of caviar.

"Mr. Roth. Walter Blake," the banker said as he held out his hand. Blake's linebacker-body threatened to send his shirt studs into orbit.

"Good to see you Walter," George said. "Congratulations on Ellie Martin's victory in the Congressional primary."

"You're one of our great customers," Blake said. "You've always paid your loans on time." The banker laughed leaving George uncertain whether this was a joke or whether Blake had checked his payment record. Was he aware of the progress for George's loan for the Grand Odyssey?

"Try to." George smiled. "That's the usual way."

"Some deal your wife's come up with. The moment Hugh mentioned it at a Board meeting, I knew it was a winner. You give her the idea?"

"The idea was all hers, Walter. Women have the ideas these days."

"We have some female v.p.'s at the bank. Pretty sharp babes, actually. What impressed me about your wife was the way she takes a plan in her teeth and runs with it. She's a greyhound who caught the rabbit. A lot of men come into the Bank looking for money for a great idea, but they don't know how to get to the market place."

Blake droned on while George considered it strange how he could be both proud of his wife and enamored with his mistress.

"What finally sold me," Blake said, "was when she lined up four doctors to make house calls. Doctors haven't made house calls in my lifetime." He gave a big laugh and George also chuckled, hiding that he hadn't known about the doctors.

"How much benefit is there for CHMO with Bonnie's business?" George asked.

"Hell, it's perfect for CHMO. If your wife takes off, this

idea will save the insurance industry hundreds of millions. She can charge good fees and still save the insurance companies a bundle. You'll notice some long faces around this room on some of the hospital people. Bonnie's business might lead to some empty beds."

"And it will lower our medical insurance premiums a wee bit also," said Tony Gagnon as he joined the conversation. Gagnon, with a more-than-healthy paunch and absolutely no hair had gone to high school with George. They occasionally met, usually when Gagnon, the head of a shoe manufacturing company, wanted George's take on a real estate investment.

"Hello Tony, I was just telling George here how successful his wife is going to be."

"Before you know it Walter," George said, "you'll have to admit her to the Hunt Club."

"I don't know about that," Blake said. "Our members come from long established companies, but George if you want to play golf here, we can put together a foursome."

"George doesn't have time for golf," Tony said. "He's too busy fighting for abortion rights. I haven't had a chance to rib you since that debacle at KQQV."

Blake looked lost, so Tony related the experience back in March debating Susan Cordry.

"George, why are you involved with something like abortion?" Blake said. "That will get you nothing but trouble."

"Shouldn't government stay out of our medical decisions

like it ought to stay out of banking decisions?"

"You're probably right, but I wouldn't touch it with a ten mile pole," Blake said. "I don't want people throwing baby dolls around my bank. If you want to fulfill your civic responsibilities, I'll get you involved with the Symphony or the United Way."

At dinner George sat at a long, white-clothed table covered with multiples of every conceivable piece of silver and glassware. He talked with Deborah Collins, Hugh's wife, over soup, salad, chateaubriand with Béarnaise sauce, roasted potatoes and onions, asparagus steamed just long enough, and popovers you couldn't throw as far as a feather. Then came speeches as the waiters cleared the baked Alaska dishes.

While he half listened to the nice remarks about Bonnie—her creativity, her willingness to jump in and solve one of the nation's largest problems, her business smarts—he thought about the kickoff celebration he was going to throw when Billie Johnson and hopefully the Wizard came to town. Sheila had been feeding him ideas—hot-air balloon rides, a jazz band, a booth with XLPOR videos—as readily as she had planned the Family Planning Center fund-raising kickoff. His big worry was that Bonnie might meet Sheila at the event.

The sound of his own name brought him back to the table. In the midst of introducing Bonnie, Hugh Collins said, "George Roth, please stand so everyone has a chance to meet the supportive husband at home." His face grew red before he climbed out of his chair. Not at being characterized like "the little man at home," but at shame for being anything but supportive. For sitting at his wife's dinner, daydreaming about Sheila Szabo.

CHAPTER 24

Mid-July, 85 degrees when George walked Chipper at 6 in the morning before spending all day with Binta and their architect. While moving around magnets on a large replica of Grand Avenue and surroundings, they allocated space for housing, retail, office, underground parking and parks and recreation. Around 7 P.M. they walked out into the lingering heat and humidity. "I'll make you dinner," Binta said. "My mom and dad are at the movies." With Bonnie at a meeting and Sheila out of town, the invitation sounded especially good.

The Browns lived in an early 20th-century, two story house in the Central West End of the city. "Make yourself comfortable while I get something started. You can set a couple of places at the card table." She led him to the kitchen and pointed to the cabinet and drawer for dishes and stainless

The aroma of roasted garlic from the kitchen made him feel at home and hungry. On either side of the fireplace, floor-to-ceiling shelves were crammed with books, photographs mostly of Binta in one activity or another, Monopoly, Scrabble, ceramics, a pair of binoculars sitting on an open bird book that sat on a tennis racket, and even a pair of fluffy slippers on top of a blanket.

"Remember Rambo?" Binta said as she bounced into the room in a pair of jeans and a button-down shirt. "My mom made those," she said as she took George's arm and steered him to the ceramic display, eight or ten figures, mixed on two shelves with a half-dozen glazed bowls and plates. "Rambo is having pups. Mom left me a note that there are three so far, more to come."

Back in the kitchen Rambo was curled under a table on a bed of newspaper and a white sheet. "There's the fourth, Binta said." Three tiny puppies nuzzled next to Rambo as she bathed the fourth with her tongue. Binta stroked the mom's back, while George held out his hand to Rambo who probably detected Chipper. He ran a finger over the pups' backs.

"You'll make a fine midwife," she said, "but no rush. Rambo should do the first mothering. The vet said not to let her eat too much placenta. A little's okay to stimulate her milk, but we'll get rid of the rest."

"Since when do you call this good-looking, female Golden Retriever, Rambo?" George said.

"George, get with it. We no longer have gender purity. Plus, Rambo is one tough daughter-of-a-bitch."

A faint odor fought against the garlic and whatever Binta was cooking. When Rambo stopped licking and began to chew on the afterbirth, George had seen enough.

"I bet we'll get six," Binta said. "Let's have dinner, so we're ready for the next."

She handed George a corkscrew and two glasses and then added the cooked pasta to a pan of sautéed vegetables and chicken. The mixture reminded him how seldom these days he and Bonnie sat down to a cooked dinner. He missed that part of their marriage.

They chatted at the table about the project, and then Binta said, "George, I'm worried about you."

"Me? Why?"

"All you do is work."

He wished his life were that simple and wished he could explain to Binta the challenges of balancing work, home and Sheila.

"You're no slouch. What are your plans when you graduate?" he asked.

"Work twelve hours a day and make a lot of money," she said but couldn't keep a straight face. "George, I don't know if you're a good role model or not."

"Probably not."

"Should I be like you and work for myself, or like your wife and start something. Or go with a not-for-profit or the government."

"Try them all. Every job I had before this one helped prepare me for the next one. Someday I might ask you for a job."

"Yeah, yeah." But George could tell she liked the idea. "Let's check on Rambo."

In the kitchen, the rear half of Rambo's body pitched back and forth on the floor as though she were riding a subway. She made little sounds from the back of her throat and greeted Binta and George with a whimper. Binta bent down and patted her side.

"It's a breach," she said. "You can see the pup's back."

"What can you do?" George asked.

"Take the puppies so she doesn't smother them. There, girl. You'll be alright. Put the pups in the living room and turn on the gas fire so they stay warm."

Binta steadied Rambo with a hand on her back, and stroked her head and neck. Rambo's spasms stopped for a few moments. Then she squirmed and jerked again.

"It's a contraction," Binta said. "George, get that towel. Grab the pup."

"You're kidding," said George who had been too squeamish to watch Bonnie give birth to their children. Binta didn't reply, and he did what he was told.

Binta held Rambo's back and head and said, "Bring it out back first."

Down on one knee he peered at Rambo's puppy-bulging labia. His khakis and sport shirt weren't great for an aspiring obstetrician. He bent closer trying to figure out how to handle the slimy transparent sack that protected the puppy without getting the blood all over his clothes.

"What do I do?"

"Grab hold. Turn off your brain and use your hands."

He shuffled his knees to get closer and slid his hand onto the tiny body.

"When she contracts, bring out the pup."

Rambo squirmed and he pulled with the towel. Damn. Nothing. He waited, while Binta caressed Rambo's neck. He'd have to pull harder, but was afraid he'd tear Rambo or hurt the pup. The tick of the kitchen clock sounded like a gang of cicadas. The fur next to his hand started to move, then stopped. He encouraged her with a couple of pats and a caress over her quivering side. Another contraction. He pulled harder. The contraction came. The tiny body moved up in the opening, but not out. Damnit. Kneeling above Rambo gave him no leverage. He had to get down onto the floor.

If he could get a grip, one more contraction might do it. He lay down onto the floor with one hand on Rambo' back, his face close enough to nurse. The two of them waited. A shudder flowed down Rambo' back. A yelp came from her mouth. He readied his hand. With extra strength—not full power but it had to be enough—yank. No luck. Harder. Out popped the sack and the puppy.

"Matilda," Binta said. "It's a girl. Grab a knife from the rack and cut the sack and get her breathing. Rambo might not be up to it."

As George kneeled with the knife, the placenta slid out, warm ooze spreading onto his hands and pants. Already a mess, and not feeling half bad about it, George finished the job. Careful of the puppy, he cut away the slick coating and the cord. Binta told him to raise Matilda above his head, then suddenly lower her, which started her breathing.

Binta sewed together Rambo's naturally-inflicted episiotomy. She pulled through the final stitch and examined her handiwork. Then she eyed George. "We've made a mess of you. I'd send your clothes to the cleaners but you'd have to wear one of my dresses." She laughed like when she had told him that Sunset Village sounded like a place old people went to die.

"Don't worry," he said. "I'll throw away the clothes."

"I'll get you a towel."

The bathroom mirror showed that his shirt was splattered with blood. Part of the placenta had dripped onto his head, streaking his hair as though he were making a run at middle-aged punk. The smell all over him had no comparable odor he could recall.

When Binta walked him to the Saab, she ignored the mess and hugged him despite his pullback to protect her from his shirt. He drove off with a sense there was something more than dinner he ought to thank her for.

CHAPTER 25

A week later the owner of a property that George and Binta wanted gave an ultimatum. Someone else had made an offer, but he would sell to George and Binta for one million dollars if they could come up with the cash and close in 10 days.

George met with Keys to discuss an advance from their partnership. "I wouldn't do it if I were you, Pard," Keys said. "We've never pyramided our projects before. That's a first step toward perdition."

"We might be okay without the land, but we need it to have a great project."

"If you do it, I'll loan you the money. You'll have to pledge your interest in our shopping centers."

George thought it over for a day. His ownership in their four existing shopping centers was worth several million. The risk didn't seem too great since they had a loan commitment from the bank to fund the entire Grand Odyssey early the next year. He could use part of that loan to pay back this loan to Keys. The Grand Odyssey was his opportunity to do something special. If the project didn't work out, the new land would still have some value as an apartment building it now was.

He decided to go ahead, but first he needed Emanuel Brown to agree to pay half, so he arranged to meet.

"We're fifty-fifty," Brown said. "I'm ok with your

preliminary budget and development plan. But now you want me to come up with half a million dollars. That wasn't the deal."

Binta and George explained where they were with the land options and this additional piece of real estate. They explained that their loan, over a hundred million dollars for the entire project, would be funded early next year, and then they'd each get their half million back.

"Is that a certainty?"

"It is unless something I can't imagine happens," George said.

"Estelle, what do you think? What would they say at the business school?"

"The business school would give you a lot of risk-reward gibberish. Forget that. You need to be comfortable. Business school doesn't teach the need to sleep well at night." George couldn't recall seeing Brown uncomfortable. The photos on the wall, their several get togethers. A few weeks ago, George needed Brown's signature and found him dressed in overalls on a job where he had joined a crew working overtime to catch up with the schedule.

"I'll do it, but if there's a problem, I'm holding you responsible, Roth. Remember, I do the construction."

"I'll have my lawyer write something up."

"We don't need to write a thing. Estelle, tell Roth he can trust me. I'll have the money on Monday."

"George, you can trust my dad," Binta said and laughed. "You really can."

George had little doubt. There was something about Brown and most of the contractors he had dealt with. They were straight forward and basic. They had immovable ideas of what was right and wrong, not necessarily reasonable, especially when it came to asking for more money because something wasn't clear in the plans and specifications they had to follow. They did what they said they'd do and thrash out the money later.

"And I trust you," Brown added.

Somehow Brown's "I trust you" sounded more like a threat than an assurance. George had never done a deal with Harry Keys without a written agreement. But Keys had found ways to avoid their agreements. George had gone along because he trusted Keys to find profitable solutions.

"No writing works for me," George said. "When it comes to our loan, the Bank will require some kind of contract between us. Let's leave it open until we know what they want."

"Ok, but find some way to limit our losses or I'm not signing any hundred-million-dollar loan." Brown stood up and held out his hand.

George extended his own and added, "Meanwhile we need some cash for the kickoff event. How about we each throw in another ten thousand."

"I'll have it Monday."

⇌

"What do you think?" Helen Roth said after George took a bite of a croissant she had handed him. They sat on his mother's patio on an August morning that would soon be too hot for outside. George had worked up a good sweat when he jogged with Chipper to his mother's.

"Okay. Not bad. I'd eat it, but if you want the reviews to say you have the only perfect croissant in town, you need lighter and fluffier."

"Dammit, I agree. I was hoping you'd say this is it."

"This is pretty good. Just not what you're aiming for." George tore off a piece of the pastry and offered it to Chipper, who lay next to his chair. These days she paced George on runs rather than chasing squirrels where there were too many trees for success. George liked to think Chipper was happier than he was with Mr. Kreuchenmeister.

"That's not good for him," Helen said.

"It's just a bite. He'll eat anything."

"My damn teacher at the chef school thinks I ought to be satisfied. He doesn't know how to make it lighter."

"Find a new teacher or get ideas on the internet." He pulled out his phone and found an article that suggested using less butter.

"Now about my lease in your Mid-County Mall. When do I get it?"

"Most of the stores aren't open at breakfast. No traffic. You'll need to be in the Grand Odyssey. People going to work. Students from the University. You can't miss there with the right croissant and other pastries."

"You won't open for another year or two, if you ever open." Which was part of George's strategy. Hopefully his mother would lose interest in croissants if he could delay her.

"Meanwhile you could get a part time job at the bread company. You'll learn store management and see if you really want to do this."

"I'm impetuous. I want a store right now at Mid-County." She laughed and said, "I sound like you when you were eight. Get me a lease," she almost screamed.

"I have a conflict of interest. Call Harry Keys and negotiate with him. Let's go Chipper. I have to get to work."

George's phone rang while he and Binta were meeting to finalize their application for a permit for the Grand Odyssey kickoff. They needed approval for a hot-air balloon and a jazz combo. The Parks Bureau still wasn't sure about the balloon in the middle of the City even though they had previously allowed one in a park further west.

He punched the speaker-phone button to answer the call. "George, this is Rabbi Isaacs, reminding you of the Temple carnival in the middle of September. Now's when you need to get that squared away."

Still focused on how to sell the hot air balloon to the City, George said, "Sure Rabbi. I'll get on it."

"What the hell are you doing with a carnival?" Binta asked after he hung up.

"Something for the kids at the Temple."

"George you have a carnival to run for adults at our kickoff. You don't have time for a kids' carnival."

For the first time he considered what he'd have to do for the Temple carnival, which he had been to when Tom and Robin were in Sunday School. There was a chair over a man-sized bucket filled with water, fixed so that someone sitting in the chair would be dumped into the bucket if the kid hit a target with a baseball. He'd need booths like one offering a trough with water, stocked with fake fish that the kids would hook and win a prize. He'd have to buy and haul drinks and treats. Binta was right. What the hell was he thinking? How could he put on a kids' carnival while trying to develop a complicated multi-million-dollar project?

By the time Bonnie walked in for dinner while talking on her speaker phone, the carnival was filling his thoughts. Bonnie mouthed "a minute or two." Her computer guru wanted another hire because of the growth of the number of providers using their services. "Will one hire carry us for six months?" she asked. With the phone on the counter, she and George hovered over the fridge, pulling out the leftover carcass from a chicken they had bought at the supermarket. "We also need stronger software," the computer woman said.

"Give me a short memo of what we need along with a budget," Bonnie said. "Price a large enough modular system so we don't need to revisit the CPU as we grow. Plan on adding the next generation software."

Meanwhile, George's anxiety over the carnival rose. When he binged on ice cream after dinner, Bonnie asked, "What's going on with you?"

"I've got this goddam carnival I told the Rabbi I'd organize. I can't do it. I already have the Grand Odyssey kickoff, the Family Planning Center fund drive, the other two boards I'm on, four shopping malls to run. This is crazy."

"You're almost shouting," Bonnie said. "This has you upset."

"You're goddam right I'm upset. Everyone's asking me to do things and I don't have time." The more he talked, the more distraught he became. "I can't do it. I can't take it anymore. Binta Brown helps, but sometimes I have to guide her, which takes longer than if I did it myself. The Archdiocese wants a booth at the kickoff, which is totally inappropriate with all the other churches in the area. The Mayor doesn't want his opponent to speak. My mother wants a lease at Mid-County Mall. Everyone wants something, and I can't stand it."

"You need to calm down."

"Yeah, I need to calm down. Wave your wand."

"George, I'm worried. I've never seen you this way. You always handle everything."

"Not any more. I'm not going to handle anything. Fuck the Grand Odyssey, fuck the Family Planning Center, and fuck the kids' carnival." He burst into tears.

"Go ahead. It might help." Bonnie put her arms around him and let him rest his head on her shoulder. After a few moments, he picked up his bowl and went for more ice cream.

Bonnie grabbed her phone and began scrolling. "I'm calling that therapist I saw back when Robin was acting out in tenth grade. See if she can help."

"Perfect, call a shrink who specializes in adolescents."

Bonnie walked into the kitchen and made a call that George couldn't follow from where he sat. He wanted to fetch the maple syrup from the fridge for his ice cream but he didn't want the therapist to hear him crying. When Bonnie returned she gave him the name and telephone number of a recommended psychologist.

"You call," George said. "I can't handle it."

Again Bonnie went into the kitchen. When she returned, she said, "The psychologist suggested you call your doctor to prescribe some anti-anxiety pills. I'll pick them up. She also said she can meet with you at 7 tomorrow if you want. She'll be in her office whether you come or not."

After Bonnie returned, George took two of the pills, He went to the kitchen to thank Bonnie, who was washing the dishes while on the phone, talking with an occupational therapist. He mouthed his thanks and headed to bed. He didn't know whether to make the 7 o'clock appointment or instead withdraw from life. He could fade into oblivion, join some ascetic order and meditate for the rest of his life.

In the morning he felt no better, but did throw on some

clothes and drove to the shrink's office. Genevieve Simpson looked about forty. She wore a white blazer over a black shirt and blue jeans, and gestured for George to take a seat in a comfortable chair from which he could easily make eye contact or not as he chose. He narrated his nightmare, much calmer than the night before, even laughing at himself once or twice. He was too calm, making him wonder whether Genevieve would understand how upset he had been and might be later that day. He concluded by saying he felt a step away from joining a monastery for the rest of his life.

Genevieve laughed, which George thought was inappropriate. Maybe he should get up and leave. Instead he laughed with her.

"You need to call the Rabbi and tell him you can't do the carnival," Genevieve said. "It's too much. Too much going on. You're not an experienced carnival guy. Ask the Rabbi to find someone else. Who did it last year? You'll do the best carnival ever when you're older and retire. Then you'll enjoy having the kids dump you into a bucket of water."

George left totally relieved. At Starbucks with a large cappuccino, life was wonderful. At five after nine he called the Temple and told the Rabbi that he couldn't do the carnival while he had so much going on.

"George," the Rabbi said. "All it takes is a phone call to the carnival company. I can do it myself, but I'm hoping I can revive your interest in the Temple, get you involved more. The carnival company does all the work, sets up the booths, brings the drinks and treats, everything. All you have to do is make the date and show up if that works for you."

George felt wonderful. He was back in charge of his life and didn't even have to renege on his promise to do the carnival. He called the company, and in less than 10 minutes, made the arrangements. As he drove to City Hall to finalize the kickoff permit, he thought about how Bonnie had taken care of him last night.

CHAPTER 26

The unpredictability of a kickoff challenged George's need for control. Added to the usual hoopla designed to create community and tenant interest were the demand to speak by the Mayor who was running for reelection, his opponent's demand for equal time, the Mayor's insistence that his opponent not speak, a potential SAVE picket, and the possibility — no, the likelihood — that Sheila and Bonnie would meet. Today felt like a tightrope-walk without a net.

Dew on a brisk September morning sparkled on the grass as Chipper followed George around the kickoff site where he greeted Binta and workers as they arrived. The rental people set up tables and chairs while Binta and George erected easels for renderings of how the Arts District would look after construction of the Grand Odyssey. Prominently shown was XPOLR.

The truck with the hot air balloon arrived. Guests could rise several hundred feet for a view while the balloon remained tethered to the ground. The balloon operator, a man in an orange jump suit, wearing a black eye patch like a pirate, glanced at the sky, and said, "Looks like the showers will hold off." They'd better, George worried. Chipper snarled at the man, but Binta, with a few free minutes, growled and wrestled with the dog until he rolled over for a nap in the sun.

At ten George raced to the airport to pick up Billie Johnson, whom he had flown in from Phoenix to play up XPOLR as a featured draw for the District. The jazz band greeted their return with a spunky version of "On a Clear Day." Shortly the first guests, including Bonnie, arrived. She had a luncheon date, and he hoped she would leave before Sheila appeared. "Don't worry about me," she said. "I'll look around while you entertain your guests."

The Mayor, dressed in a stiff herringbone jacket, a size too big as though it were an older brother's hand-me-down, stood alone until he saw George and sprang like a hungry grizzly. As he got close he broke into a big smile. "My speech is twenty minutes."

"Because it's the middle of the day, Mayor, maybe you could abbreviate parts," George said. He made a mental note to put the Mayor last when many guests will have left.

Eyes turned to the arriving Porsche and George's mother. When George greeted her, she handed him a super-sized bag full of assorted homemade breads, each in a baggie tied with a red ribbon. "I'll look after myself," she said after she delivered the bread to the caterer. "Let me know when it's my turn in the balloon."

The jazz band picked up the tempo with the alto-sax-players' version of "Take Five." To George's surprise, the kickoff was presenting no problems.

He felt proud of having The Grand Odyssey on track. He and Binta had convinced XPOLR to put the project ahead of Denver, had applied to tidy up the zoning and other permits and were processing architectural documents. Unlike his previous deals, he had done it all, with Binta's help and without Harry Keys. He wondered if Keys would accept his kickoff invitation.

Profit projections weren't great for the first two years, but by then they should achieve full occupancy for the residential and office space. Ahead were many challenges, dealing with the architect, Emanuel Brown assembling subcontractor bids, handling construction snafus, and mostly finding the tenants. He loved the challenges. They would absorb ten, twelve, fourteen hours a day and allow him to ignore the minor aggravations that occupied him when he didn't have a project. He took a deep breath, as though to take in their achievement, and instead got a taste of local heat and humidity. The clouds approaching from the southwest would provide a welcome shield from the sun.

Harry Keys and Sheila Szabo arrived at the same time and walked together from the parking area to the caterer's tent. Sheila's beige suit, bought casually off the rack, fit as well as Keys' custom tailored, gray pinstripe. They dressed like a team of IBM representatives. Obviously, Keys had introduced himself and was charming Sheila, probably with a story at George's expense. Sheila said "hi," and like George's wife and mother, moved on.

"Nice minx, your family-planning bimbo," Keys said.

"She's a successful professional, Harry." His eyes

followed Sheila who had connected with his mother. Could Keys suspect something?

"You're still stuck on the details, Tiger," Keys said. He studied a rendering of the Grand Odyssey. "You've done a nice job. Now comes the tough part."

The roly-poly owner of Shepherd's, a family restaurant, joined them.

"Hi Ernie," Keys said. "You going to move down here?"

"Could be."

"A good spot for you," Keys said.

"Good to have your support," George said to Keys. Over Keys' shoulder he noticed his mother and Binta, about to climb into the balloon basket.

"Just telling the truth," Keys said. "Besides, better for you to have good tenants if I have to bail you out and take over."

"Bail me out?" George laughed. He looked again at the balloon, but Linda Taylor from the University walked up and said hello.

"Too bad our students aren't back for your carnival," she said.

He introduced Keys and Taylor. Over Taylor's shoulder, he saw the balloon ten feet off the ground, thankful that Binta was with his mother. "Have some drinks and sandwiches."

Invited guests and passersby began to fill the area. George greeted all he could. He became aware that the clouds had arrived with a warm breeze that gently pulled at the balloon, now 200 feet in the air. His mother was gesturing to the pirate.

He looked around to check on Sheila and Bonnie, but instead saw a white stretch limousine, a Moby Dick of stretch limos. It stopped and sat—no one emerged—like a just-landed spacecraft full of aliens studying the earthlings. A tuxedoed driver smartly hopped out of the limo and opened the rear door. Two black men in dark business suits climbed out. Wow, Terry and Tom Allen.

"We're looking for Binta," Terry said. "She told us we shouldn't miss this event."

For three years George and Keys had unsuccessfully courted the Allen brothers. They owned the fastest-growing, sport-shoe retail chain in the country, with stores they coupled with a rock-climbing venue. George and Keys had never convinced Terry, a former pro football player, or Tom, a former pro basketball player, to even visit one of their sites. George considered Binta with a mixture of surprise and awe.

"Welcome to the Grand Odyssey," George said. He walked them toward the easels where he explained the outstanding demographics for the site, plenty of nearby young residents plus well-to-do students.

"When do I speak?" Mayor Martin butted in. Fortunately the Mayor recognized the Allens, whom George introduced, and the Mayor began a sales job for the City, which he handled fairly well.

As his mother and Binta approached, Tom Allen said, "Here comes a hottie."

"Pardon me." Helen Roth said in feigned offense.

"Excuse me, Ma'am. Certainly wasn't referring to you."

"For six months no one's had the decency to call me a hottie. I thought you'd broken the drought."

George introduced his mother, which gave the opportunity to change the subject.

"I love how you get around," Terry said. "Maybe you'd teach some of our challenged customers."

"Any time, young man."

Binta offered some ideas for how Terry could improve his jump shot.

"Maybe you'll demonstrate," Terry said as Binta escorted them toward the renderings.

George introduced his mother to the Mayor whom he told speeches would begin in forty minutes.

"A nice party," his mother said as George walked her toward the cars. "Maybe this shopping center business is more fun than I thought. That pirate in the balloon is crazy but he knows how to tell a story. And Miss Binta Brown, wow, she adds some class."

A blast of wind blew across his face as he returned to the party. A storm was approaching with the temperature at least ten degrees cooler than before. The kickoff might end because of the storm. Dust from a nearby softball field was blowing in tight circles, first in one direction and then another. Maybe they'd avoid the Mayor's speech. He turned and saw the balloon a hundred feet in the air. The cabin and the ropes leaned toward the east. Fortunately the ropes were attached to heavy stakes. Up above, the pirate was shouting words George couldn't hear. Three people were in the balloon. George looked away to see what other problems a storm might cause. Suddenly he looked back. "My God," he said. In the balloon with the pirate were Bonnie and Sheila.

Drops of rain spattered the dust as people walked toward their cars. Somewhat to the west lightning played across the sky. Bonnie and Sheila would be in danger if they didn't get that balloon down right away. That crazy pirate. He should have known better. A friend had recommended him after his kid's birthday party. George ran under the balloon and tried to hear what the pirate was screaming as he waved his hands in loops. The ropes strained to hold the cabin. When lightning flashed again, George counted, waiting for the thunder. A thousand-eleven, a thousand-twelve, a thousand-thirt— There it was. A little over two miles, maybe 5 or 6 minutes away. The balloon was a perfect target.

Then he realized that the pirate wanted the assistant to let go of the ropes. It was their best hope. They'd never lower the balloon ahead of the storm. George ran up shouting, "Cut the ropes. Let go of the ropes. Let them blow to the east." Not so easy because the line strained against the wind. He screamed for the assistant to pull some slack so he could loop the rope around the stake. It must have taken a whole minute to free one rope. Then they ran to a second. More lightning and thunder, nearer.

The rain came hard. People were running. "Mr. Roth, Mr. Roth!" George heard a voice over the sound of wind and rain.

"What?" he screamed without letting go of the second rope that was almost loose.

"Mr. Roth." The Mayor shouted into his ear. "When will we do my speech?"

"Mayor, help unwind this rope." When it came loose, the balloon tilted away from the two remaining ropes.

Binta Brown and Tom Allen were working the third rope, so George ran to the fourth where Billie Johnson and Terry Allen were struggling. Billie couldn't get traction and kept sliding on the grass. As the third line came free, the last line absorbed the full force of the wind. The balloon cabin tilted more. Bonnie and Sheila were struggling to hold on. George joined Billie and Terry but they couldn't get the line over the stake. "George and I will pull. You unwind," Terry screamed at Billie. Together the two men pulled. George dug in for traction. Like in a tug of war, in those Superstar competitions. Tom Allen and Binta joined them. Together they pulled until Billie flipped the rope, once, twice. The line went slack. The balloon lurched and then blew wildly toward the east.

George stood drenched, next to the dripping Binta Brown. A mixture of black, blue and purple clouds wove in and out of each other like swirling cars in a carnival ride. Billie and the Allens stood with them, staring after the balloon. George shook from exertion and fear for Bonnie and Sheila. Even as he focused on how to track the balloon and find Sheila and Bonnie, the storm reminded him of the Wizard of Oz. Would a wicked witch greet his wife and mistress?

CHAPTER 27

"What a show," Binta said.

"That was my wife and—"

"Your wife. My God," Terry Allen said.

"I have to find them," George's hands shook.

"How?" Binta said. Her dark skin sparkled through her soaked dress.

"They might hit an office building," George said.

"Won't happen."

"They'll give you a call when they land."

But what if they don't land? What if they fall?

"The Pirate knows what he's doing," Binta said. "Let's get out of the rain."

"I'll take you to the airport," George said to Billie.

"Let's go to the office," Binta said to the Allen brothers, "We can talk about a lease and, George, get your mind on something else after you get back from the airport."

"We'd do a letter of intent," Terry Allen said.

With Sheila and Bonnie in danger of being killed, he couldn't imagine working on a tenant deal. He'd trade for a safe landing even if Bonnie learned about Sheila and him.

"Not this afternoon," he said. They agreed Binta would show them the rest of the area. They'd get together in the morning.

From the car George tracked down a meteorologist who told him the storm was headed toward Indiana. "They'll land somewhere in the I-55 corridor, but I can't tell you where. The FAA might have picked them up on radar." But the FAA was too busy routing planes around the storm. They had no record of a balloon.

George changed clothes at home and microwaved a cup of soup that he drank on the way to the office. The charcoal sky reflected his mood. Would they be okay. What would Sheila say once they landed, if they landed? Would she describe the mole underneath his belly button? For an instant he imagined high voltage wires snaring the balloon and killing them both. For a dreadful moment their deaths seemed a relief to George, and then shame bullied the thought from his mind. He blamed himself. If I hadn't — Harry Keys walked into his office and interrupted his thoughts.

"Joyce told me about Bonnie and the minx." What did Keys know? "They'll be okay. Too bad your kickoff took a hit."

"At least we avoided the speeches," George said.

"Sometime I'll tell you about Binta Brown's father. I heard he's into drugs."

"You're stuck on the stereotype. He's a respected businessman,"

"They say he's one tough hombre. Just trying to warn you, Pard."

Typical of Keys to cast a shadow on what George had accomplished without him.

The next hour and a half reminded George of an anxiety-laden wait he had endured one day in fourth grade. He got nailed at lunch, sneaking away to the corner store. The principal wanted to send him home, maybe send him to an alternative school. George sweated in the office, biting his nails, while the principal tried to find his mother. But his mother never arrived, and at three, when the bus was loading, he slowly walked, head down, past the secretary, and out the door.

The call came from Bonnie in Springfield, Illinois. "Thank God you're safe," George said after she related they had just landed in a field near a shopping-center. Perspiration flowed down his sides. They were about to buy some clothes and check into a motel near the shopping center to shower and change. George noted the address.

In his SAAB, worry replaced relief. His jaw ached like he had bitten a seed in a supposedly-pitted olive. He tried to ignore it and wondered which was worse: The two hours Bonnie and Sheila would spend together while he drove to Springfield, or the two hours while the three of them drove back.

Damn. Construction on the bridge over the Mississippi. The overpass backed up west of the river. Listening to the radio as he crawled ahead, the talk shows were more nuisance than distraction. Music made him impatient. Just as he broke free at the funnel point, his phone rang. He almost didn't answer because he was concentrating on the barricades and little orange cones that channeled traffic through a series of choices. Once he maneuvered to what looked like the correct lane, he pushed the button.

"Hi, Sweetie Pie," a woman said through the static.

A crank call. He almost hung up, but something in the voice made him say, "Who's this?"

"You wouldn't guess in a hundred years, Sweetie. I was up in a hot air balloon with the nicest woman."

"Sheila," he whispered. "I thought you were with Bonnie. Where are you?"

"I'm safe and sound in Springfield, Illinois, Sweets. A terrible storm blew our balloon away. Me and this woman whose husband owns shopping centers."

"What are you doing, Sheila? Where's Bonnie?"

"We're doing okay. We bought clothes, rented a motel room, the other woman's in the shower."

He rapidly approached one of those temporary signs with arrows pointing in both directions. The pavement was too slick to stop. He had to turn or hit the sign. Which direction? A car on his right, offered no choice but to swerve left without a full look behind. Fortunately there was no car.

Instead he heard, "Honey?" He cleared the sign.

"Sheila, is Bonnie with you?" Before she answered, he heard his wife. "My husband can give you a ride unless you want your friend to come get you. The two of you could keep this room for the night if you want."

"Honey, you don't have to come get me. This nice lady's husband will give me a ride. Unless you want to come up and spend the night."

"Sheila, cut it out and be careful."

"I love you too," she said and hung up.

When it struck him that Bonnie had taken a motel room with Sheila before he had, his irreverence seemed as bad as his adultery.

For a hundred miles to Springfield, he tried to get his arms around his life. So far Bonnie knew nothing, but how long could that last? Maybe she was too busy to want to know. The fact that he cared about Sheila made his betrayal greater than if sex were the only attraction. During the past five months he had felt more alive than any recent time. Sheila had brought him to life. Or had it been the Grand Odyssey? What about the phone call? How could she have called him in front of Bonnie? He loved Sheila's wackiness, but the call was reckless.

Since the Botanical Garden, some defense mechanism had muscled most of the guilt from his mind, but now it was back. Even if Bonnie didn't figure out his betrayal, today was a monstrous warning?

By the time he passed Springfield Lake and began fumbling with his GPS for the motel, he knew he had to do something but didn't know what. Take a business trip, visit prospective tenants in California, take a few extra days, think through his ridiculous life.

Bonnie suggested he wait outside the motel room where he imagined Sheila's underwear drying next to Bonnie's. He paid the bill while they stuffed their wet clothes in plastic laundry bags. On the trip back Bonnie couldn't stop talking. The balloon ride was the most exciting experience of her life. "Once we cleared downtown, I knew we'd be okay." Then she couldn't say enough about his mother who had suggested at the carnival that she hire older people to visit their patients, straighten their homes, read to them, even pray with them. Like a home hospice.

Bonnie, her back against the front door, her feet on the seat, her chin on her knees, talked for ten miles about how much she admired Sheila. "It's incredible that you started your own business while raising your daughter. You know so much about health care." Bonnie gets her kicks with Sheila, just like he did.

A subdued Sheila sat in back. "You already know more about home healthcare than many of the men I've worked with know about their own businesses. Many are specialists who know one thing, but if you talk something else like insurance, they call their insurance person, and if you talk billing they call their numbers person."

"Sheila thinks insurance companies and the government will reimburse the kind of services your mother suggested for older people."

George pictured Sheila and Bonnie ballooning over Illinois discussing insurance reimbursement. Better than if the two of them had analyzed his so-so sexual technique while comparing orgasms. He sometimes worried Bonnie was faking hers. "He doesn't do it for me," he pictured her saying to Sheila. Inappropriate thoughts never used to flood his mind.

He nodded and pretended to concentrate on the road. Dullness spread through him as though the dentist had filled his body with Novocain.

"We have to find a way to network," Bonnie said. George heard something new. His wife's certainty and enthusiasm. Speakers at the Hunt Club had praised her qualities and he hadn't recognized the person they were talking about. Now he saw it. What if she succeeded and no longer needed him? That prospect comforted him at first. She'd have her business, he'd have Sheila. Maybe there'd be no conflict. They'd all agree. Then fear overwhelmed the relief. Bonnie wouldn't forgive him no matter how successful she became. And what the hell did he want with his own life?

"You're on a roll," Sheila said. "You don't need a consultant."

"We'll work together," Bonnie said. "Help each other get business. Maybe put together a package insurance companies can provide their corporate clients. Like how to help employees assist their aging parents without overwhelming the employee's job at the office."

"Great idea," Sheila said. "Employees looking after aging or sick parents is a leading cause of absenteeism."

Bonnie had jumped to a different level, to a concept that went beyond either her or Sheila's business. Remarkable. Bonnie was poised to leave him behind.

"You're into big things," Sheila said. In the mirror she looked like a tired child after an all-day outing. Like any minute she'd ask if they'd be home soon. "I kind of like my little business the way it is. But I'll refer my clients to you."

⇋

The next day George went to Sheila's for breakfast. After she handed him a mug of coffee and a bagel, he said, "How could you pull that telephone stunt from the motel? I was weaving through construction barriers, trying to figure what was going on with you and Bonnie."

"I was falling apart, which makes me crazy. I thought I was over that kind of thing, but we were almost killed. I'm sorry."

He put his hand over hers and said he understood. He realized again that Sheila meant more to him than sex. Recently life seemed split between sex with Sheila and companionship with Bonnie, complicated by occasional sex with Bonnie and growing connection with Sheila. Being in love with two women might tear him apart.

"I've got news for you," Sheila said, "maybe good news for all I know. Your wife is in love with her business and the idea of being in business. Being the boss. That's a real high for a woman who's spent her life picking up her husband's underwear."

"There's a difference between love and infatuation. Wait until she encounters all the problems."

"You haven't been listening, George." Sheila spread a thin layer of raspberry jelly on her bagel. "She's handled loads of problems already. You need to think about what you want.

If you don't court your wife soon, you'll lose her and be stuck with me."

"I am thinking about it."

"I feel terrible about calling you yesterday. In the car. I knew it was crazy. I like Bonnie, and I'm jealous."

"Jealous?"

"She has you."

They ate the bagels and hardly talked. Once again, unlike the day before, George felt comfortable with Sheila. He too was jealous, jealous of Bonnie's business. After they finished, Sheila moved to his lap. She worked her hand into his shirt.

"Not now," he said. "The Allen brothers are at my office to sign a letter of intent."

Sheila unbuttoned her blouse.

"I have to get back."

She opened the front of her bra and dropped it off her arms.

"You're beautiful," he said, "but—" She put a hand over his mouth and used her other hand to squirm out of her pants and then her panties.

"We don't have time to do it right," George said.

"Then we'll do it fast."

CHAPTER 28

On the way to the office, George thought, I'm like a compulsive eater swearing off food after each gorge. However, Sheila was more than an obsession. Would giving her up save or end his life?

Binta and the Allens were waiting with a bucket of champagne. After they signed the letter of intent, had their toasts and the Allens left, Binta said, "Your mother called. With you not here, she asked what I thought of a croissant shop at…" — clearing her throat and raising her eyebrows — "at the Grand Odyssey."

"She's determined to carry out that nutty idea."

"Nutty?"

"You met her yesterday?"

"She told me I had class. She's hip, man."

"She's seventy-seven."

"She's spunky. The kind of person I'd like for a partner, George."

"So why don't you do it with her." His mother might have a chance with Binta's help.

"I'll think about it," Binta said, "and while I'm getting in bed with your mom, you might think about getting more in bed with my dad."

"We're 50-50. What more are you talking about?"

"He's a contractor. Contractors have low opinions of real estate developers, like we're all fluff, no brick and mortar.

He says he might not sign the loan for the Grand Odyssey."

For several weeks George stewed over Sheila's warning that he was losing his wife to her business. Some days he felt relieved not to be solely responsible if their marriage came apart. Like having Sheila was okay because Bonnie was going to leave him. Other days, when he had no appointments, he sank into a funk. As if Bonnie were already gone. He stared out the window and wondered where she was. What she was doing.

Had business become Bonnie's entire life? He looked for signs, but they were together so seldom he had little opportunity. One morning at breakfast he said, "How about going for a pumpkin Sunday?" Every year for Halloween when the kids were little, they had gone to a farm out in the county near the Missouri River.

"Great idea," Bonnie said. "Something has come up I need to talk with you about."

"Like what?"

"Wait till we're in the car and have a little time."

George wondered if she were going to ask for a divorce. "Something has come up" might be some man she met.

Sunday on the way to the farm, Bonnie unbuttoned her suede vest as the heater warmed the SAAB.

"What's going on?" George asked. "How's the business going?"

"Great, maybe too well. I've lined up most of the hospitals. They resist at first. I tell them what's best for the patient is best for us and them. I tell them the hospital's a lot better off recommending us than having the insurance company turn down their bill. Most of the hospitals have gone along, reluctantly, but St. Matthews tried to screw me."

"How's that?"

"We met and they acted real nice like they were going to use us. At the last minute they announced they were going to begin a competitive service. I told them none of the other hospitals would use St. Matthews' home service for fear they'd lose the patient next time he goes into the hospital. If the hospital didn't work with us, we'd have no incentive to encourage their patients to go back to St. Matthews. They backed down."

"You're good at hardball."

"Gave me a high." Bonnie's voice contained the same glee George felt when he landed a tenant, secured a loan, opened a shopping center. Sheila was right. Bonnie was a love-smitten entrepreneur. He felt like asking where he fit with her success but realized he didn't know where Bonnie fit with him. Right then George felt prepared never to see Sheila again, to re-nest with Bonnie. Success was the ultimate aphrodisiac.

"You said something has come up." Traffic had backed up a quarter mile from the farm, as families decided it was time to prepare for Halloween.

"Two venture capitalists from Silicon Valley contacted

me. I had to look on the internet to see what a venture capitalist is. They said they were prepared to buy a part of my company for two billion dollars."

George spit a mouthful coffee back toward the thermos.

"I know." Bonnie said. "I can't believe it either. They want me to go national. They said that if I don't do it, someone else will, and take over our territory."

"I've read about venture capitalists," George said. "They're awash with money, and they can't find enough ways to spend it."

"They would be on my board of directors. They'd provide management input, which could be a good thing."

Kids in the car in front of them were leaning out the windows, waving at Bonnie and George. Bonnie's news made George feel more like a child in today's world of business. All he did was build a simple shopping center or mixed-use development. They waved back.

"They say my salary ought to be at least a million dollars a year and that I should have stock options for more ownership." Fortunately George was between coffee swallows. Bonnie was laughing.

"I've read about some of the more notorious venture capitalist deals," George said. "They financed one company that kept lowering its prices to drive out the competition. By the time they realized they were going broke, they were losing over $200,000 an hour. An hour. The entrepreneur, the Bonnie in the deal, was way over the top, buying vacation homes with money he borrowed from the company, driving twin Bentleys, flying in 2 company jets with a stable of pilots and flight attendants, and more. Meanwhile the venture capitalists didn't want him to turn against them and give them a bad name in the entrepreneurial world, so they kept putting more and more money into the company."

"They want to fly out here next week."

"How do you feel about it?"

"Flattered of course. It's an ego trip. I pictured myself on the cover of Fortune Magazine. But I'm scared. I remember the story of Icarus flying too close to the sun."

"The business world is full of Icaruses. I remember some banker bragging about buying Countrywide Lending a few months before his company needed a bailout. But what do you want? What's important to you?"

"Right now I'm having fun. I could stay just as we are. But if these guys are right, someone will drive me out of business. I feel I ought to explore this. See how it goes. After all, a million dollar salary wouldn't be all bad."

George grew silent as he pictured Bonnie building her empire. His first reaction was excitement. He pictured giving up shopping centers and becoming her assistant, responsible for something, though other than getting an annual physical, he knew nothing about healthcare. Wanting to be his "powerful" wife's assistant was the part of him that had made him a good number two behind Keys.

His second reaction was to ask, "How are we doing? Are we growing apart?"

"I think about that and I don't think so. We're a typical midlife marriage, no kids around. Now's time we either branch out in new directions or hunker down and start to grow old."

"I guess so," he said, aware that some of their married friends had broken up at midlife.

"We should keep our eyes on making time for each other. That's why I loved your idea to come out here today."

They parked and walked toward the farm. They needed nothing, not even a pumpkin for the kids, though carving one themselves might provide a connection. The farmer had constructed a fort, protected by straw witches and gremlins. Kids, a little too old to look for pumpkins, played "Indian" and stormed the fort, the rambunctious ones giving tomahawk blows to the "settlers." George recalled the bones at the Kreuchenmeister farm and how dealing with Harriette Dunn and No Name had shown him the injustice of how Native Americans were portrayed by white culture.

They walked to the fields where the pumpkins lay in long rows. Hundreds were stacked in a thirty-foot-high pyramid, protected at the top by a ferocious witch on her broom.

"What a nice day," Bonnie said.

"Can you enjoy it without thinking business?" George asked.

"I can. I have a hundred things to do, but if I can't take off one Sunday morning a month, something's wrong."

"I keep thinking about a construction schedule."

"You've always lived your work," she said

"Is that where you're headed?" They had arrived at a petting zoo. Kids reached over a wire fence to pet rabbits, puppies and kittens. For the first time in years, George missed having small children.

"I don't know," Bonnie said. "I want to work my buns off to create a successful business and contribute to healthcare. I never dreamed how big it could be. Everyday I'm pumped full of endorphins."

George envied her. After taking a job in real estate, he had made few choices. He had fallen into his life, first with Barnes, a developer who went bankrupt, and then with Keys. George had taken each opportunity because it came along. Shopping centers were not like an irresistible puppy. He had worked to earn money, because men were supposed to find jobs and go to work. Bonnie had gone to work because the children were grown and she wanted to move beyond being a housewife. He'd be sick of it too. She had struck gold and rode an endorphin high, while he developed shopping centers because he didn't know what else to do. Accomplishments provided only short-term endorphins.

At the produce stand they bought some apples, squash and a jug of cider. Back in the car he had no idea what to do next. The trip was over. Some minor Grand Odyssey tasks could eat up part of the afternoon and football on TV the rest. It was a perfect afternoon to make love. He and Bonnie hadn't had sex for over a month. He wanted to do it but was reluctant to risk bringing it up.

"That's as nice a morning as I can remember," Bonnie said.

"Delightful." He put his arm across the back of the seat and massaged the back of her neck, where she liked it.

"Mmmmm," she responded. He caressed her cheek and she trapped his hand against her shoulder.

"What now?" he said.

"How about going by the supermarket? We can pick up salads at the salad bar, take them home and do some work."

He almost said, "Let's go home and ravish each other," but was afraid Bonnie wouldn't want to. A salad sounded good. He would go over his long list of tenant prospects and assign each one a priority. He'd plan a California trip, including extra time to figure out his life. Maybe Sheila would go with him.

"Salads sound good," he said.

CHAPTER 29

Tom, a teacher in Chicago, and Robin, a senior in college, came home for Thanksgiving. Tom brought his girlfriend, Addana, a fellow teacher, originally from Nigeria. George took a few days off, but Bonnie was so busy making her venture-capital deal that she left the meal-prep to George and the children. Robin put together a complex dressing recipe she had read on her flight, Addana made jollof rice, a dish from her homeland, and Tom took on the turkey. George consulted The Joy of Cooking, and then cut some string beans for a casserole. After he couldn't find the mushroom soup in the cupboard, he cooked the beans in the microwave and tossed on some dry, shaved fried onions. The dinner was perfect with all five of them sharing stories and laughs about the food prep with less-than-usual results, compared to a Bonnie-prepared meal. George relished having the family together, even though the short visits reminded him that once he finished developing the Grand Odyssey, he'd have little to do.

Sunday morning they all drove to the airport. The children headed back to school and jobs. Bonnie was off to New York to close the sale of 40% of her company to the venture capital firm in exchange for one billion dollars to her and an eventual two billion infusion into the company. The New York advisors and law firm she had hired had improved the deal, urged her to take a five million dollar salary, which she had rejected. The Board insisted on one million plus another million for incentives. They all said goodbye at security, and George headed to his gate for a flight to Los Angeles.

He planned to meet for three days with possible retail tenants. Sheila would fly out on Friday so they could spend a long weekend together. This plan to meet in fantasy land as temperatures dropped in the Midwest seemed idyllic. It was not to be.

On Monday George lacked enthusiasm when he presented Grand Odyssey plans and renderings to leasing people. Tuesday he cancelled appointments and instead walked the beach in Santa Monica. Pumpkin-hunting with Bonnie and then Thanksgiving with the family made him feel like his life was upside down. Sure, he could rationalize his relationship with Sheila—Bonnie had become mostly unavailable, would become more so as she developed a national business, and sex with Sheila, begun as a flirtation, then an infatuation, had recently evolved into a meaningful sharing of parts of their lives. It all had seemed somewhat natural.

No longer. As he wandered through the Greek and Roman art at the Getty Villa off the Pacific Coast Highway, he realized he was a monogamist by nature. An exhibit explained that Zeus was promiscuous in order to seed the Mount Olympus gods. George's linear brain might be right for "seeding" a shopping center with tenants, but not for the complexity of a wife and a mistress. He watched people balance work, social media, telephone calls, all with one hand on their mobile phones while carrying a designer-coffee in the other hand. He couldn't do it and didn't enjoy trying.

Sheila and he shared a warm hug outside the LAX terminal before driving south toward San Diego and the La Jolla resort where they planned to spend the weekend. Camp Pendleton, a stark Marine training ground, gave a taste of California desert. What would it be like to develop a shopping center out here where people wandered outside among stores year around.

In La Jolla they sat in the sun on their balcony and watched surfers in the ocean. One caught a large wave that upended her half way to shore. Sheila kicked off her shoes and leaned back. George couldn't relax.

"I have thoughts to share," he said.

"I can tell."

"I need to end our affair."

"Tell me more." She stretched her legs but didn't turn to face him.

"I'm torn apart. I was okay juggling two relationships, but that was before you've become so important to me. Being drawn to both of you pulls me apart."

"I also have something to tell you," she said. "Let's go for that walk you promised and we can talk some more."

The beach from La Jolla to Delmar ran next to a cliff on which sit the Scripps Research Institute, the University of California at San Diego and a takeoff site for hang gliders who circled above. The tide was coming in so they removed their shoes to walk past several places where the cliff jutted into the ocean. Sheila was subdued, mostly quiet, no laughs, no jokes. "What are your thoughts?" George finally said.

"A lot of feeling about this past year. Our time together has been so important to me. The way you dealt with that meter maid and that poor girl after the bomb made me like you from the start. I cherish our sex at the Botanical Garden, an all-time experience. I appreciate your reserve while being emotionally obvious. I feel a connection I never felt with my husband."

"We're no good with a casual affair," George said.

"I even love your wife, which is what I need to talk about. She offered me a job as the head of strategic planning."

George stopped and turned toward her. "We don't need Sherlock Holmes to see the problem."

"Nor NCIS. I'm leaning toward telling her yes, but I can't work for Bonnie and have sex with her husband. Your reluctance to continue solves my dilemma."

"The job is perfect for you if you're willing to give up your consultant's independence."

"She offered stock options which could guarantee my security, make me financially independent."

Quietly, they walked, so slowly George thought he could count the grains of sand. Sheila pointed to the spout of a far-off whale. For a better look they tried to climb the cliffs, which proved too steep. Owners of the houses at the top had raised their stair-ladders to keep wanderers out.

"I'm so sad," Sheila said. "In a simple universe, we might have moved out here to paradise where people walk on the beach in the middle of the winter."

George had nothing to add. A feeling spread through his body from the same sadness he couldn't find words for.

"And I'm so happy," Sheila said. "I'm going home to a beautiful daughter, a wonderful job and a chance at security I've always chased. I'll be stuck in the Midwest, looking for a mate who's like George Roth, maybe one who's a little looser, though you've been learning."

They decided to have sex one more time, a chance to celebrate what had been an important part of their lives. They had learned more and more about how to satisfy each other, taking their time, prolonging the experience. Sex with Bonnie, always satisfying, had evolved little from their shy beginnings. If they could find the time, it might evolve more. Anticipation of change ahead both worried and excited him.

CHAPTER 30

Binta graduated first in her class a semester early, having taken a heavy course load including classes during the summer. Investment bankers, consulting firms and venture capitalists, including the one working with Bonnie, were recruiting her.

"What do you think of your daughter?" George asked Emanuel Brown as they mingled in the University gym after the speeches and diploma procession. Pamela Brown, Binta's mom, had left to finish cooking for the guests coming to celebrate.

"You want the truth, Roth. White people don't understand work. Estelle has a job offer for $200,000 a year. Starting out. They tell her she'll be running a team of consultants in two years, and make more money."

"Sounds like a good deal." George recalled the brash young woman who had told him that "Sunset Village" sounded like a place where old white people go to die. She already had a consultant's air of authority. "You and I can't afford her any longer."

"She won't learn what work is."

"She'll have 14-hour days, 6 or 7 days a week."

"In an office. Playing with numbers and what she calls 'strategies.' That's not work. Not what you did when you started out, I'd bet."

George recalled his first job, a high-school summer "construction" job, relocating a stretch of interstate. The boss asked George to figure out what it cost to move a cubic foot of dirt. Bulldozers pushed freight-car-sized dirt-movers that scraped up the earth, delivering it into their huge beds, before running it to a dump or "save site." Certainly not real work to Emanuel Brown.

"She also says she wants to help my mother make pastries, maybe earn a thousand dollars a year." George laughed.

"That's more real than being a consultant."

"You want her to join your business."

"I raised her to kick butt, not numbers."

"Maybe she'll come back. Meanwhile she'll get good experience."

"She wants to see how far she can go pushing money and ideas around. She also wants to finish developing your deal, the Magnificent Odyssey."

"I'd give her part of my share of our deal. How about you?"

"She can have the whole damn thing as long as I'm the contractor and don't have to sign any loan papers."

"If we tie down enough of the risk, that would work," George said. "I bet your tax advisor can give you some loopholes to increase the benefits."

"Tax advisor? Are you kidding me. I use a part time bookkeeper. Real work doesn't have loopholes."

"Hi dudes," Binta said as she walked up. In addition to

her gown, she wore a big smile. "Are you plotting the rest of my life? My dad's favorite pastime."

George felt like a second father to this woman he had become close to while working together. He had been a mentor, and she had been his mentor. While he developed strategies with feints and misdirection as learned from Keys, Binta made a direct approach. Her voice and demeanor said she expected people to accept what she was asking. If they didn't she easily asked why and then met their objections. On occasion, she'd say, "I understand. We just won't be able to make a deal."

"We are plotting your life," George said, "but I suspect you'll make some edits. What are your plans?"

"I'm going for the big bucks with the consulting firm. They've given me permission to finish what I'm doing for our deal."

"I expect you to be on top of our deal," Emanuel Brown said, "at least until I get my half million back."

"Also I'll help with your mom's croissants. Speaking of whom, I hope you're bringing her to our party."

"Wouldn't miss it," George said. Along with all the good feelings of the day, George loved the image of his mother bossing around a five-hundred-dollar-an-hour consultant who was about to lift a tray of croissants from the oven.

December was a productive month. George signed

letters of intent with retailers; Bonnie signed up medical providers for her home-health delivery system; Sheila settled into her new job, planning with Bonnie and key executives, the steps they needed to establish the business around the nation; and his mother developed the technique for what she called "the perfect croissant."

"Really good," George said one morning between Christmas and New Year's when she had summoned him and Harry Keys for breakfast and her sales pitch to lease space in the Mid-County Mall. "We always have a vacancy somewhere. Why not?"

"Full rent," Keys said.

"Three free months and percentage rent for the first year," Helen Roth said. She held up a book entitled, How to negotiate a retail lease. "Better for you than having vacant space. Plus we'll attract people in the mornings."

"On their way to work, not to go shopping," Keys said. But he said it with a laugh, and eventually offered to give it a try when the right space became available.

The first week of January brought a deep freeze and bad news that threatened everything. Sears, which was one of the anchors in all of his and Keys' shopping centers, was closing its operations in the metropolitan area. Online sales and other consumer attitudes were turning large shopping centers into retail graveyards. Sears was contracting nationwide.

Keys was off to New York to convince them that his and George's shopping centers worked as a trade area for Sears. George didn't have much confidence Keys would succeed.

Hank Smoltz at River National Bank called and asked George to come for a meeting to discuss the bank's loan commitment for the Grand Odyssey. Binta was in New York finalizing her job deal, so George put on a business suit and went alone.

As before Smoltz escorted him up to the executive offices. Once off the elevator, George asked, "Where's the men's room, Hank?" It wouldn't hurt to keep the bankers waiting.

"I guess it's okay to use the executive rest room." Smoltz pointed. "Around the corner."

George set his briefcase under the marble vanity. At the urinal, pages from the day's Wall Street Journal, taped to the wall, stared back at him, including an article about Sears' contraction. The door opened behind him. A man walked to the adjoining slot, looked to his left toward George and without recognition, said, "Good afternoon."

"Spencer," George said. Smith looked haggard. "I understand we're meeting today."

"Ah, Mr. Roth. Excuse me for not shaking hands."

George glanced over the low, narrow partition at Smith's long, fleshless, shaking arm, coaxing performance. Smith shook a little harder. He was having trouble making it work. George finished but remained at the stall to add to Smith's discomfort. They stood side by side facing pages of bond and interest quotations and a story about a CEO going to jail for fraud. Somewhere the bank had found an almond air freshener that made the bathroom smell like a rose garden.

"Terrible news about Sears," Smith said.

"Not unexpected. They'll probably keep an appliance store at our centers."

"We're concerned about your centers."

"We'll be able to convert most of their space to higher rents. Those centers are all under permanent loans. We don't owe the bank a thing."

"Your Grand Odyssey loan is based in large part on your personal wealth, which is in those shopping centers." Smith apparently couldn't converse and shake at the same time. "With these closures, we have no idea what your shopping centers are worth. Maybe nothing if smaller stores move out. We can discuss it in my office."

"It's an opportunity to reposition the centers. We have a commitment from River National, Spencer. You can't just walk away from a commitment." George imagined telling Emanuel Brown that his half million was gone. Smith, back to shaking, flushed the urinal, as though the rush of water would open the valve.

"The commitment's based on there being no material change in your financial condition before we fund the loan. A change couldn't be more obvious."

Just then the door swung open and in walked Walter Blake.

"Hey Spence," he said.

"Walter, say hello to George Roth."

"Roth, we've read about your wife. She's a real power. We increased her loan and told her not to worry about paying principal, interest only." Now both Blake and Smith were shaking.

"I'm here because Spencer wants to go back on your commitment to fund the Grand Odyssey in the Arts District."

"Ah yes, a good project. What's the problem, Spence?"

Smith explained the anchor store closures and nodded toward the Wall Street Journal article on the wall.

"Who needs department stores," Blake said. "George, you're going to have your wife co-sign the loan, aren't you. No problem with you both on the loan."

"I was about to explain that to George," Smith said as he tried to rotate his head between Blake to his left and George almost directly behind him at the washstand.

Smith either urinated or got tired trying and joined George. After he dried his hands he also dried the counter and hitched himself up so he sat on the marble, his thin daddy-long-legs hanging over the side. They both watched Blake's back, George in the mirror and Smith directly.

Just then the door opened and in came a bewildered Hank Smoltz.

George had heard enough. He didn't want to argue about whether the bank could cancel its commitment, which sounded like something for lawyers. He was ready to leave, but making his way through Smith at the vanity, Blake at the stall and Smoltz between the two of them was like trying to scramble between a defensive lineman and a linebacker. At the door he said, "I doubt my wife's backers would allow her to sign onto a development deal. I'm going to count on the commitment, gentlemen. I need to meet with the Mayor who is also counting on you going forward."

"Stay away from abortion," Blake called after him. "Now if I can just get my goddamn pecker to work."

CHAPTER 31

Mid-January and George still hadn't discussed his loan with Stan Dalton, his attorney. Dalton had spent 3 weeks in New Zealand, and George waited until his second day back, only to learn he was out of the office. Dalton's mobile went to message. Every minute or so, George hit redial to give Dalton a message of urgency and hoped to catch him between calls. "Damn mobile phones," he muttered. He felt sick of his life, one-day plane trips, out on the 6:45, back at 9:30 so he could make a 7:00 A.M. breakfast meeting the next day. He and retailers emailed lease documents because Federal Express was too slow. He wanted to remove the verb "to email" from the language. "Fuck redial buttons," he said out loud as he stabbed the button once more, and once more got Dalton's message.

The ring of his own phone yanked him out of his daydream. "Glad I reached you," Sheila said. Since their trip to California, he had seen Sheila once at the Family Planning Center, where they were scheduled to meet in a week to wrap up the previous year's fund drive. "We need to talk. Can we do the wrap-up now at my house before I leave for the office?"

"Sounds good but I might get sidetracked if I reach my lawyer. An emergency with the bank."

Predictably, Dalton called just as he drove into Sheila's driveway.

"Stan, River National Bank is reneging on my loan commitment." George summarized the conversation at the bank. "Can they do that?"

"Maybe. Probably. Trouble is even if they can't, by the time you fight it in the courts, you'll need a different loan or your deal will be dead."

As Dalton talked Sheila walked out of the house and across the lawn. She wore a light-weight, hanging dress that blew in the cold wind, which she didn't seem to mind.

"George, are you there?" Dalton said. "Did I lose you?"

"I'm still here, Stan. "

Sheila was acting like they were still together, doing a whimsical dance in front of his car. She was making signs like she was playing charades. She pantomimed holding a large ball, like a globe, in front of her. With cupped hands she swung her arms back and forth above the hood. What the hell was she saying? She pointed at George and then herself and then to her stomach. And then swung the arms again.

"I've got to go," George said.

He realized what Sheila was telling him. The phone dropped from his hand. He switched it off and pushed open the door. By the time he got to his feet, the phone was ringing but he let it go.

"You're pregnant."

She nodded.

"How could that happen?"

"You're old enough to know." She laughed again.

"You know what I mean."

"It must have been in La Jolla. My diaphragm's always worked. You know what they say at the Family Planning Center — no method is 100 percent."

The complications to Sheila, Bonnie, and his lives ran through his mind faster than an emailed tenant lease, leaving him speechless.

"Come take a look, Sweetheart." Sheila pulled up the shift to just below her breasts, baring her belly and crotch that was covered by a translucent thong. Houses were spread out in the development but the trees in the front yards had lost their leaves. Any neighbor on either side could see Sheila's strip tease, not to mention anyone who drove by. "Looks like my ovaries didn't get the message that we were breaking up. Ovaries might be like the brain. The left side's rational and the right's creative. It was the right's turn."

George's greatest adolescent fear had been that he would get a girl "in trouble." Even when he was a virgin, he had awakened some nights from a dream in which his girlfriend was pregnant.

What George couldn't explain was why he felt good. He certainly didn't want another baby. He wasn't one of those types who married two women in different parts of the country, with children running all over the place. Obviously Sheila would get an abortion and he'd recognize his own responsibility and go with her to be supportive. It would work out, but surely this rational plan wasn't what was making him happy.

Inside she pulled him to the couch, no longer the contemplative, rational Sheila of La Jolla. Once again George felt joyfully connected to unpredictable, uninhibited, crazy, fun-loving Sheila. Gone was the reality of the bank. Gone was Sheila's absence from the last month of his life.

Replacing the month's reality was a fantasy that Bonnie falls in love with someone else, he marries Sheila, their infant daughter sleeps through the night as soon as they bring her home from the hospital. He had her halfway through medical school when Sheila said, "I know we can't have the baby. Before I have an abortion, I want to dream a little."

Relieved, his back sank into the softness of the sofa. With Sheila's craziness, he half expected her to want to have the baby. "We can at least enjoy the fantasy," he said.

The enjoyment lasted about a day until it ran into his overactive mind. The fetus was not a human being as the right-to-life people claimed, but an early stage of developing into a human being. A daughter or son whom he would love, and who, if he were a decent father, would love him. Yet, regardless of how he felt, their having a baby would be a mistake.

He had learned to keep his reactions under control. He appreciated his mother's preposterous behavior but "not for me." Still his brain censor couldn't erase the images of fatherhood, a baby in his arms. He tried, unsuccessfully, to ignore the images.

⇌

Seventeen inches of snow accompanied the decision of the owner of an independent coffee shop in the Mid County Mall to move to Hawaii. The next day the owner requested permission to sublease. George called his mother, who agreed to take over the location as soon as she could get someone to shovel her driveway.

George cross-country skied to the Center, a once-in-a-lifetime city experience on city streets with no cars. A bright sun and white landscape reflected off windows, and patches of fog lingered where the 10-degree air sat on the warmer ground.

Over cappuccinos the shop owner and George agreed that the lease would immediately be turned over to Helen Roth. The owner would pay 3 more month's rent and be released from the following 15 months. On Wednesday people were able to drive, and they agreed to meet at the shop at three in the afternoon when business was slow.

Helen would need someone to run the shop and best bet was Marie Turnbridge, the coffee shop's assistant manager. Marie was skeptical, maybe after watching Helen move through the store to a table in the mall. "I should be looking for a more stable long-term job," she said.

"We're as long term as you can be," Helen said. "When I decide to retire in another hundred years, you can have the shop."

"That's fine, but what if the shop doesn't work out?"

"It'll work out because we'll have the best coffee and croissants in the County."

"I'm sure you will," Marie said. "We've always been the best, but the word never got around."

"I'll get the word around. There has to be some benefit to having no legs. The newspaper ran an article about me last year, and George knows the general manager at KQQV who could give me an hour of call-in."

"Not enough people get their coffee when they come here to shop," Marie said.

"Not when they find out they can drink it with the best croissant this side of Paris. Before long, George, you'll pay us to be here instead of us paying rent."

"Sorry I'm late," said Keys as he pulled up a chair from an adjacent table. "Sounds like I arrived just in time. Did someone say, 'no rent?'"

"Like an anchor tenant," Helen said.

"We could use one after Sears moves out."

"Sooner the better. I wouldn't sell my croissants in any place that has a Sears & Roebuck. They used to be something, but they can't afford to print their catalog. Good thing I still have my old long johns for a day like today."

Marie looked back and forth following a dialogue that probably seemed to come from a different planet. "I should get back to work," she said.

"Would you consider giving it a try?" George said.

"It's a lot of responsibility. I'd need a raise to take over as manager."

"Of course," Helen said. "And you can have half the profits."

Marie smiled but refrained from saying what she thought half of the profits might be worth. They discussed logistics of the takeover and shook hands before Marie went back to the shop.

CHAPTER 32

George and Sheila stepped off the elevator at the fifth floor. To their left was the fire exit. To their right an armed guard. Sheila gave her name which the guard located on his list. He invited them to empty their pockets and walk through an airport-style metal detector toward a door.

A teenager in the waiting room didn't look up while a woman in her forties, next to a man, gave them a welcoming glance. The teen flipped through "Elle," turning each page with a sweeping arm that came close to hitting the woman next to her, probably her mother.

Sheila clutched George's arm and gave him a look that seemed a mixture of appreciation, adoration and fear. "Guess the first thing I noticed when I saw you today?" she said in a lowered voice, not quite a whisper. Several people peeked up and then back down at their magazines.

He ran an index finger under his nose to be sure a hair hadn't appeared despite his regular trim since Sheila had joked about his nose hairs.

"Last time you asked me that, a bomb exploded," he said, careful that only Sheila heard.

"A bomb is exploding inside me right now."

George glanced to see if anyone had picked up her words. Apparently not. "My guess. The first thing you noticed was my body?"

"Your body's terrific but the first thing I noticed was that you came with me today. In the midst of all you have going on, including your mom and your wife, you took the time. Brought me here, to the Family Planning Center, where people know who we are. You care about me."

He squeezed her hand. His arms tingled as if under siege by a colony of gnats that also ran across his belly. Two weeks earlier he had wondered about taking Sheila, anonymously, to a clinic out of town. He couldn't do it. The Family Planning Center was one of the safest, if not the safest abortion clinic in the country. He didn't want Sheila to take chances. His concern reminded him how much he cared about her. He loved Bonnie, their memories of parenting and making a family as well as his admiration for her business success that had brought her to life, albeit while taking her further from him.

"Toni, Sheila and Vicky, please come with me," said a young woman wearing an open beige cardigan over her nurse's uniform. She had a slight smile, to George a look of reassurance. George rose with Sheila, gave one more squeeze and within seconds was alone with the mother and the other man. Each looked at the others. One smiled. They returned to their magazines.

George reread the instructions he had received in the mail from the clinic. He wouldn't see Sheila for several hours. The nurse would take her to a counselor. They would talk. Confirm that Sheila wanted an abortion. She'd go to another waiting room, then to blood testing and other tests before finally she'd have to wait once more. The abortion wouldn't take long, but then there was a recovery room and another room where patients got themselves together before leaving. He wished he could be with her, but the social worker had explained over the telephone he couldn't. A "significant other" — George was an SO — had once destroyed part of an operating room because he opposed abortion.

George looked over a draft of the transmittal he was submitting to lenders to replace River National Bank. Submitting to local lenders would get back to River National, which might reconsider since the Grand Odyssey was a prestige project in the City. He couldn't concentrate on the papers. Words danced on the page in nonsensical patterns. He put the papers back into his pocket. Where was Sheila now? Maybe into blood work.

"SO counseling is about to start," said the nurse in the beige cardigan. George, the mother and the other guy who had been with Toni followed the beige sweater who turned out to be the counselor.

"Some couples tell us it's harder on the men than the women," she said.

George smiled thinking she might be right, but he wouldn't admit it.

"Boys aren't encouraged to show their feelings so when they grow up, many really don't know how to. Many are experiencing grief and don't know what to do with it."

George and Mr. Toni nodded. George could hardly

remember his father, who had been killed when he was 7. Grief was what his mother had shown, crying all day and then trying unsuccessfully not to cry in front of George in the days ahead.

"If you can express your feelings of loss when your friend or relative comes out of recovery, it will help her not feel alone and might help you too."

Beige Sweater made him feel comfortable. He pictured Sheila, brave but frightened. That's how he saw his mother these days, putting up with days of uncertainty in medical offices. His own lack of patience couldn't tolerate regular doses of the health care system.

"Another way to be supportive is to take an active interest in your friend or relative's aftercare." Sheila would be okay. It ought to be emotionally easier for her at forty-four than for a teenager or someone who wanted to raise a child.

"Perhaps this is an opportunity to talk about birth control."

But they didn't. Instead the door opened. Another nurse or at least another person in a nurse's uniform, looked in, first at Mr. Toni, then at him. "Mr. Roth?" she said.

"Yes?" He jumped up.

"Would you please come with me."

"We're almost finished anyway," Beige Cardigan said.

He followed the woman. Eleven forty-five, his watch said. Too early. Sheila had been gone only an hour and a half. Something was wrong. She should be in the procedure room right now. No way she could be out of recovery. They walked along a series of corridors reminding George of the maze at XPOLR in New York. Most of the corridor doors were closed. Inside one that was open sat someone at a desk, inside another two people were talking. A sign outside a room read, "Community Relations," and behind its glass door a group was meeting. It was quieter than a library.

Everything George had read, everything he knew from years of involvement said that abortions were safe. Complications were more common in childbirth than abortions, and hardly anyone died in childbirth. Sheila's trusting and vulnerable face flashed before him. What if something happened to her. He'd never forgive himself. He never should have kissed Sheila almost a year ago, and then become a virtual spurting teenager.

"Where are we going?" he asked.

"Primary counseling," the woman said.

That's where they dealt with difficult cases. What would they tell him that they couldn't tell him in SO counseling? Then it struck him. Something was wrong. Very wrong. Panic rose inside him. It was serious. He pictured Sheila being whisked off in an ambulance. His bowels contracted like when he had been led to the principal's office in fourth grade. Pressure settled in his chest and head. How many corridors did this place have?

They turned another corner and walked into a cluttered office. Straight ahead was a gray metal desk full of files, phone, stapler, pictures—he could hardly see the table top.

An almost knee-high waste basket had spilled papers onto the floor. Dust danced in the rays of sun coming in the window. George looked to his left. There, waiting, was Sheila. Sheila? She looked okay. She had made it through the procedure. The muscles in his shoulders and back melted.

"Hi, George," she said. She acted fine. Much better than before the abortion. She must have dispensed with the bullshit and gotten right to it. Just like Sheila.

Then he remembered Beige Cardigan's advice. Show his own grief. "It was the right choice," he said. "But it's still hard to lose what might have been our baby."

"Oh George, you feel the same way. I was so worried you wouldn't."

"I feel the grief too," he said.

"But George, you don't have to. I changed my mind. I didn't go through with it. I don't want an abortion and I'm so happy you agree."

"What? That's not what I said. Of course I want an abortion."

"Which is why you're both here," said a woman whom George noticed for the first time. "I'm Marilyn Darnton, a primary counselor. The three of us need to talk."

"We've talked about this already, Sheila."

"I've changed my mind."

"Why? What's changed?"

"I want the baby."

"You haven't decided a fetus is a human being, have

you?"

"And if she has," Marilyn Darnton said, "what's wrong with that?"

"If you thought that," George said to Marilyn Darnton, "how could you work here?"

"I don't think an eight-week fetus is a human being, but it's okay for other people to believe that and for their belief to affect their choice."

George sank back in the chair he couldn't remember having sat in, his body a balloon that had lost its air. Of course it was okay for someone to believe a fetus was a human being. But damnit, he wanted this pregnancy behind him. With everything going on in his life, he didn't need another seven pounds, six ounces. He calmed himself and said, "I thought we had agreed."

"I know you want an abortion," Sheila said. "I thought I wanted it too. But lying on the table, under that sheet, with my feet in those stirrups, I knew more than anything I've ever known, I want to have this baby."

"Has Sheila told you about her and me," George said to Marilyn Darnton.

"Some. Would you like to tell me more?"

"You know I'm married to someone else?"

Marilyn said, "Kind of hard to duck out to change diapers." And to Sheila, she said, "I'm wondering if keeping the baby is like keeping a link to George."

"I work for George's wife so I have a connection to George. I just want the baby even if I raise her myself."

"The two of you have some sorting out to do. Maybe the three of you. Your wife also."

"We shouldn't impose all that onto a baby," George said.

"That may be something over which you have no control." Marilyn Darnton smiled. George was struck by her demeanor. She didn't rise to the bait. She effused a sense of calm, the absence of crisis. Her smile was a twinkle that said there was humor even in this mess. "You're not going to answer all the questions here today, but let me make some suggestions that might help."

Help. A lifeline from Marilyn Darnton. His body was here but his mind was somewhere else, sinking, unable to respond. He could pull himself together for a business crisis like his loan, but the idea of telling Bonnie he was fathering a child with her director of strategic planning? Better to just disappear.

"You shouldn't decide your life issues under pressure. If you're going to have an abortion, it would be safest before the sixteenth week. You're already too late for mifepristone and misoprostol, the abortion pills. So you have some time to decide. You could have the baby and still decide to give her up for adoption. Meanwhile you can start to process how you feel about having a baby and about each other. We can help with counseling or you can get private counseling."

"We should do that, George."

"And you have some things to think about too, Sheila. At your age there are extra risks that the baby will have a birth defect. Does that matter to you? Could you raise a child with Down's syndrome? In your ninth week you can get a test called corianic villi sampling, which is like amniocentesis but can be done earlier and with quicker results."

"I'll do that. I'm willing to have an open mind, George."

"There's another thing you can do. You can even do it together if you're willing, George. Pretend you already have this baby. We used to tell teenage girls, who thought taking care of a child was glamorous, to carry a raw egg everywhere they went, pretend it's the baby they have to take care of. You could do that. Or get a doll. Change its diapers. Find baby sitters if you want to go out."

"Wonderful," Sheila said. It was a relief to see her laugh. "I still have my favorite childhood doll."

"My business is a mess without a loan. I can't sit around playing dolls."

"I'll sit with it during the day. For now I'll tell Bonnie I might use it in a strategic planning session. You can come evenings when Bonnie's out of town. We'll love it, even if we decide not to have the baby."

"What do you have to lose?" Marilyn Darnton said as she rose and held out her hand.

CHAPTER 33

"Why do you need my help?" Mayor Thomas asked when George called. George had contributed to both of the Mayor's campaigns, the first that he lost and the second he won. George had served on a panel advising the Mayor and Board of Alderman on changes to the building code. He had a casual, friendly relationship with the Mayor.

"River National Bank is trying to revoke its commitment to finance the Grand Odyssey." George explained the situation. "Finding a different lender will cause too much delay, we'll lose some tenants including XPOLR, a big draw. Costs will go up and the budget won't work. I'd probably lose my partner and have to kill the development." An exaggeration, but George wondered whether he'd want the deal after reworking the numbers. He didn't want a loser, which would be like a drawn-out death, as compared to the explosion if he lost Emanuel Brown's half million.

The Mayor responded and set up a meeting at City Hall. Walter Blake at the Bank said he'd send Spencer Elliot Smith, but the Mayor said, "No, you have to come." The City deposited funds at River National, which gave the Mayor some clout.

A late-January thaw had arrived, and wanting some fresh air, George arrived early to get a hotdog from the food cart in front of the courts building. The cart owner was the daughter of the women who used to sell hot dogs back when George was in law school and working as an intern at one of the downtown law firms. He recalled the blind man who ran the candy and cigarette shop in the courthouse and somehow could feel the difference between dollar bills and larger bills when making change. Today's meeting contrasted with the simplicity of his life back then. He asked the hot-dog woman what she thought about moving her cart to Grand Avenue when the Odyssey opened. "Pretty good, nearer my home."

At one o'clock the Mayor, Walter Blake, Emanuel Brown, Linda Taylor from the University, and George sat down in the Mayor's office in City Hall and exchanged the usual niceties. City Hall dated back two centuries and was modeled after the Paris city hall.

"You're part of this community, Walter," the Mayor said to Blake. "There's nothing wrong with this loan you agreed to make. The sun doesn't rise and fall on Sears & Roebuck these days."

"We're good with the loan as long at Mrs. Brown and Mrs. Roth sign along with their husbands."

"You want an earful," Brown said. "I'll gladly bring my wife to your office. She doesn't sign anything, not even the list of chores around the house she gives me. I ignored the list once, and she delivered it again by certified mail."

"Don't let your wife near mine," the Mayor said. "Roth, how about your wife signing?"

"That would violate her agreement with her partners,

and run afoul of papers she's filed with the SEC," George said. "She can't do it." And, if Sheila decides to have the baby, my wife might not be my wife. "But all my interests in 4 shopping centers stand behind the loan."

No one spoke for what seemed like minutes. The office had the usual trappings of power, including a photo of the Mayor with the President, another with the Pope, a commendation for having chaired the Conference of Mayors.

"This is an outstanding development, Walter," the Mayor said. "You don't need the wives. You've got the husbands, which will keep their attention plus Roth's shopping centers and Brown's businesses. What's the problem?"

George had first driven the Arts District with Binta Brown because he enjoyed being with her. She had presented the kind of dream and optimism that all projects require to get off the ground. As he worked with Binta and made a deal with her father, emotionally he was motivated as much by the possibility of doing something different and fun than by making money on a successful development. This had changed. Each piece that Binta and he put together captured a part of his ego. To fail now felt like the end of his career. Shopping centers were changing. Entrepreneurs now repositioned old shopping centers, instead of developing new ones. Bonnie was a billionaire. Even if they stayed together, without the Grand Odyssey he'd become "the little man at home" keeping dinner warm for when she got out of a meeting.

Blake's voice brought him back to the meeting. "I understand all that, but we have legal restraints too. Our Board of Directors has rules about net worth of borrowers and spouses signing for loans." This brought smiles around the desk because everyone knew the Board of Directors did whatever Blake told them to do. He must be getting desperate.

"Walter, we have a Board of Trustees at the University," Taylor said. "We've made concessions because this project can change the City. We're tired of the national news saying we're one of the highest crime areas in the country."

"Which is one of our problems with this deal," Blake said. He couldn't keep from looking at Emanuel Brown when he said this. White people, probably incorrectly, assumed that Blacks were responsible for the high crime statistics in this central area that divided the Black north side from the white south side. The bank had "raised an eyebrow" at George and Binta's inclusion of affordable housing, which somewhat diminished the deal's economics. Binta had looked Spencer Elliot Smith in the eye and accused him of equating affordable with Black, which Smith, of course, had denied.

"More than a century ago," Taylor said, "the bankers and other city leaders dropped the ball. Chicago rather than we became the center of the Midwest."

"Back when local bankers led the nation with red-lining," Brown said.

"Hold on. That may have been then, but not now."

"We have the chance to regain some prestige," the Mayor

said.

George kept his mouth shut. For once it felt good not to be the one trying to convince a potential tenant, cajole a city council, convince a Mr. Kruechenmeister to sell his land. Instead he sat back and watched someone else take the hits.

"You see this kind of development in Silicon Valley or Los Angeles," Taylor added.

"The heartland for liberals," Blake said.

"The heartland for money," Taylor said.

"What's wrong with liberal?" the Mayor said, and then laughed as though to tone down the talk before they entered the culture war.

"I have an appointment," Blake said. He looked uncomfortable, unused to not calling the shots. "I have my doubts, but I'll talk with some of the other banks about syndicating the loan. Maybe we can get it done." George was surprised, as the banker walked out, that he didn't tell George to stay away from abortion.

CHAPTER 34

The National Association of Family Planning Providers determined that George and Sheila had run the best local fundraising campaign of the year and asked them to make a presentation at their annual meeting in New York. The invitation provided a perfect opportunity for the two of them to "parent" Sheila's doll. Sheila's first trimester of pregnancy, when abortion is simplest and safest, ran through February, so she needed to make a decision shortly.

They booked a suite and an adjoining room. "You take the suite, Honey," Sheila said. "Easier for you to do the night feedings."

For the first time in his life, George realized that parts of his life were finished, irretrievable. If he were single and 29, he'd beg Sheila to marry him. He'd think owning four and a half shopping centers was for old farts. He'd want to think like Binta Brown rather than merely admire her acrobatic mind. At 50, his metaphysical DNA had changed. He had a wife and two children. The Mayor was supporting his deal. He'd find a bank to lend him over a hundred million dollars. These realizations told him now was the time to enjoy this life. In 20 or 30 years he could open a croissant shop and look back on today with nostalgia.

He gave the bellman twenty dollars and asked him to switch their names on the rooms at the front desk so his calls would come to the suite and Sheila's to the adjoining bedroom.

Sheila removed Pandora, her name for their "baby," from a box in which she had poked three holes, and gently set her on a table. She retrieved a box of gauze squares, "clean diapers," she said, some wipes and some instant whipped cream, "the formula." We change the diapers eight times a day." She dedicated the top drawer of a chest of drawers to be the "bassinet."

"Here, I'll show you how to change her."

"I'm not brain dead yet," George said. "I remember what it was like to change a diaper. And by the way, the middle-of-the-night feedings had been blissful, on the sofa with a warm, limp body sucking away at the bottle. I'd doze off with Tom nestled in the crook of my elbow, his head on my chest."

"I hope Pandora is equally gratifying."

"Let's talk about a real baby. That's what we're here for, what having a baby will mean for our lives. And especially your life since it's you who has to decide whether to have a baby. Like who will look after her while we're both at work?"

"Pandora will do just fine. Debbie had daycare and she's doing well, better than I'd expect for a teenager."

"And speaking of that we need a sitter for our presentation tomorrow morning."

"We're going to pay someone a hundred dollars to spray whipped cream? You won't have to worry about your Grand Odyssey because they'll lock you up." For the first time in the year since they met George bristled at Sheila's laugh.

"You can't pretend our baby doesn't exist whenever it's convenient."

"Go blow it off," Sheila said with a grin. "You call if you want a baby sitter."

"Sheila, it's you who want a baby."

She called all three women from the concierge's list. On the third she said, "Just a minute," and shoved the phone toward George. "Mildred here wants to bring her toy fox terrier. You talk with her."

He put his hand over the speaker and whispered, "Sheila. This is serious." And then, "Thanks, Mildred, but not this time."

"We can take Pandora in the box. She ought to hear her parents in action."

"Listen, dammit." The room filled with silence. Something must have told Sheila not to laugh. She sat in the fake leather easy chair and fumbled with her left earring, while cupping the right in her hand so it wouldn't fall to the floor. "It's not 'Pandora.' If you have her, she'll be a real person. It's time we talk about that."

Sheila unzipped her dress and pulled it over her shoulders, all with a huge sigh.

"You want a thoughtful conversation with your clothes off?" he said.

"Oh George, you sound like you're chairing a business meeting. My clothes are tight because of Pandora or junior or whatever you want to call her." She sat back in the chair, her tumescent tummy a reminder they weren't just playing. A real person would develop inside Sheila. Some people, not just the crazies who had bombed the Family Planning Center, but some well-meaning people thought Junior was already a human being. He wondered if they were right and wished there were some God-like test for when humanhood began, a test that would satisfy both sides of the abortion fight one way or the other and make the battle go away. "Sit down," she said, pointing to the couch.

"We need to be serious, for one afternoon," he said.

"Of course it's serious. I'm just being me. I'm excited to have the baby."

The telephone rang and without a word between them, they agreed not to answer. After five rings, it stopped.

"I know you're excited. Babies are beautiful and they're fun. They're also a hell of a lot of responsibility." He got off the couch and walked back and forth past the TV, the bureau that no longer seemed like a bassinet, and the brown Formica table that sat next to the window.

"I'm not a starry-eyed teenager," Sheila said. "I'm 40, I've raised a child and I know the responsibilities. I'm entitled to enjoy it if I want. Sit down. Relax."

This time the phone seemed to reach the fourth or fifth ring before George heard it. He tossed his suit jacket onto a chair and loosened his tie. Why did he dress like this in New York anyway?

"Aren't you ignoring our problems?" he said.

"Like what will happen to my job and your marriage?

The baby's not a problem. She'll be fine no matter what we do."

She was right, of course. The baby would be fine with Sheila as a mother. Sheila could go back to consulting.

His marriage? He would tell Bonnie about their affair when he got home. He had no idea whether he'd still have a marriage, whether he'd want a marriage to an absent spouse who was fully engaged in her business. Meanwhile he'd be caring for a baby in his fifties, going to PTA meetings in his sixties, attending college graduation at seventy-two. His arm sometimes ached from six years ago when he last played catch with Robin.

People ran down the hall. Most of the delegates at the family planning meeting were in their twenties or thirties. He pictured the wild dances they would do tonight when the band came after the banquet, maybe the same dances his new daughter would learn if she came to be. Twenty years ago George would have danced with them. Tonight he'd mostly sit.

Sheila bolted straight up when the phone rang again. "Maybe we ought to answer it," she said as she unhooked her bra. George ignored the ring and tried to ignore her breasts, which had grown.

Sheila sat back and said, "Charlie and I had Debbie when we both were trying to establish our careers. Even though we did what every young parent did—middle of the night feedings, Saturday morning at the playground, school plays—we gave work the priority. This time I want to treasure every moment. Parents need to treat their babies special. Not every moment. But lots. Especially at first."

"A child ought to be wanted by both parents."

"Preferably," she said, "but maybe creation requires two just in case one's not on board. And besides, I know you well enough to know you'll be a loving father. You'll love the experience. If your marriage ends, we'll be a couple. I'd like that."

He was running out of steam. Instead of convincing Sheila not to have a baby, she was showing him how good it would be. He had been nervous around Tom, his first, and then Robin because she was a girl. He could relax with Junior.

Sheila stood up and stretched and said, "The big question is when do you want to tell Bonnie? And do you want to keep living with her? I love you, sweetheart, but in some ways you're irresponsible."

"Irresponsible?" If she were trying to goad him, she was succeeding. "Who made the reservations for New York? And for the abortion? Who has to get a loan or be a failure after years of hard work? And who will help support our child?"

"Yes, you're great at tasks. But responsibility means thinking about things and making choices. Choices based on your beliefs and values. You just let things happen."

"Like what," he said, the defensiveness in his voice competing with the anger.

"Like when we first had sex, it just happened. And when

we didn't break up at the Botanical Garden, it was my idea. And it's okay for Bonnie and me to fly in a balloon as long as she doesn't find out."

"You think it's better for her to know?"

"At least think about it, worry about it. Take responsibility. Make a choice."

"My choice is for you to get the abortion."

"To erase our mistake. You want an abortion to make life easier for you. Not because our baby would be uncared for."

"Your mistake, with your diaphragm. Unconsciously you wanted a baby."

Sheila got out of the chair and walked to the fridge where she removed the whipped-cream spray, shook the can and sprayed a handful into the palm of her hand. She approached where he sat by the TV and before he could react, smeared it in his face. "Try some formula, you bastard. It's pretty good."

The whipped cream flowed into his eyes as he peered at topless Sheila standing in front of him. His lashes stuck momentarily when he blinked. The unusual smell reminded him of when his mother used to spray some Redi-Whip on his birthday cakes. He scooped some off his face and rubbed it around Sheila's mouth. She let it drip onto her tongue and then into her mouth. George spread more over her stomach and breasts.

"Okay, George. If you want war, ..." She quickly pointed the spray down the front of his pants and let loose.

"I'll give you twenty minutes to cut that out," he said.

"You should be so lucky."

He gathered her into his arms. Sheila felt wet and sticky, like sex on a hot sweaty day. Her hair smelled of whipped cream..

"Let's clean up and go for a walk," she said. "We'll be safer in public."

Glistening she walked off to her room. Before closing the door, she leaned back and said, "George." And when he looked up, she said, "I'm going to have the baby. We don't need a baby sitter and we don't need the rest of the whipped cream."

George took a shower and returned to clean up the living room. As he rubbed the wet floor, he felt excited. He realized he wanted Sheila to keep the baby, not have the abortion.

At that moment he heard a key in the door as though someone were trying to get into the wrong room. After two futile attempts, the door swung open.

There stood a bellman with a suitcase. Behind him was Bonnie.

CHAPTER 35

"Bonnie?" Dressed in a charcoal gray suit over a patterned silk blouse, she looked like she had arrived for a board meeting.

"I tried to reach you but no answer. And then the front desk tried. When you didn't answer I convinced them to let me in."

"What's wrong?"

"Not a thing. I have a meeting tomorrow downtown so I thought we could share a room and a little time. Maybe I can catch part of your presentation." Her animated, business-woman voice compared to his memory of her housewife face—the worry lines, the wrinkled brow, the solemn mouth—when, for example, she fretted about the kids' college applications.

"I never thought—"

"The surprise will make it better. And you were intuitive to get a suite." The mention of the suite jolted George's thoughts back to Sheila. She'd appear any minute. What could he do? His mind, never great at the start of a crisis, raced to find a solution. It raced too fast, like a cassette on play and fast forward at the same time. He had to keep Sheila out of here. The quickest solution would be to walk into Sheila's room and tell her. Too risky. What would he tell Bonnie? That there was a meeting going on in there? Might work. Better to call Sheila.

"Are you Mr. Roth?" asked the bellman.

George had forgotten the man. He fished into his pocket for a tip and said he'd take care of the bag.

"Thank you, sir. A phone message, sir." He handed George an envelope with Bonnie's phone messages.

"Let's go for a walk," Bonnie said. "It's a glorious brisk day."

George looked out the window to confirm the glorious day. He nodded his agreement though all he saw were tall buildings.

"Sheila has the room next door," he said. "I'll tell her you're here and that we're going for a walk."

"Sounds good. While I freshen up, ask her to join us." Bonnie removed her suit jacket and pulled a sweater from her suitcase, a folded-hanging type of bag she could carry onto airplanes. When they used to travel together, she carted at least two checked bags, and half of what she brought stayed in the bags. Until now, when she traveled on business. She had seldom wanted to go along on his business trips.

He knocked on the door to Sheila's room. Was he really unable to make difficult choices as she claimed? With Sheila certain she would have the baby, he was ready to tell Bonnie about their affair, which was a difficult choice.

Sheila opened the door, and he told her about Bonnie's arrival. "I'm going to tell her about us and the baby."

"Ok," was all she said. "

A good way to tell his wife that he had been

unfaithful escaped George. Just tell her he told himself. When Bonnie came back into the room, she greeted Sheila and mentioned the walk.

"First, we need to talk," George said. "Last year before Sheila went to work with you, we had an affair that's been over for a few months."

"What. You what?" Bonnie said. She sank onto the sofa, ran her hand through her hair. Sheila and George stood in silence. He didn't know whether Bonnie was about to lose her temper or fall apart and begin to cry. She did neither. Instead she said, "I'm flabbergasted and at the same time, not surprised. An affair I can understand. I turned down an offer myself because I'm too busy with one life without living two. Besides, I'm having an affair with my business. But why are you telling me?" She gestured for Sheila and him to sit.

"After it was over," George added, "Sheila learned she's pregnant."

"You're not going to have an abortion?"

"I want to have the baby," Sheila said.

"As the father I'd be involved. It's not something we could keep secret. I felt I should tell you once Sheila decided to have the baby."

"How selfish. Did you consider the child's complicated world. Did you consider in vitro."

"In vitro success is low at my age and an abortion would make it lower."

"How about an abortion and then an unmarried

surrogate father. George has no monopoly on fatherhood."

George was stunned by Bonnie's logical progression of options, her rational reaction to such an emotional matter. She took a deep breath, looked from Sheila to George and back again, and for a moment rubbed her eyes. Her animation George had observed was no longer there, as though it were a rush of adrenalin that ran its course. She looked older and like she wasn't getting enough sleep.

"Let me tell you about my affair" she said. "I need to develop and make a counter proposal for a Pittsburg hospital that wants too much money. One of our nurse practitioners in Denver has made inappropriate sexual advances on other employees. I need to fire him properly under the law. We're licensed in 45 states and face obstacles in 5 more. I don't have the infrastructure to deal with these things, which are not what I should be doing anyway. I need to hire people, and my advisers tell me that hiring is the hardest job to get right. Half the people won't work out. I have two new board members from the venture capital firm, who keep me on the phone an hour a day, sometimes more. They have bad ideas I have to ignore without alienating them, and they have good ideas I don't have time to implement. And now comes my strategic planning specialist, who is doing a great job, and tells me she's had an affair with my husband. I hope you're not considering leaving the company. Right now you have us focused on our objectives and we can't afford to drift while I replace you. I have a husband I haven't paid sufficient attention to, to realize he's having sex, probably a lot of sex, with someone else. I've been propositioned several times, but I don't have enough time. I ought to be a real estate developer so I can have more fun. In any event, I'm in no mood for a divorce. We may be going public and it wouldn't help to add a divorce to the filings with the SEC. George, when you get home, move into Tom's room. Meanwhile, tonight you can sleep on the couch out here. I'll take the bedroom and leave early tomorrow." She found her sweater and walked out the door.

CHAPTER 36

George stared at a painting, actually a print, in his office that purported to be a Paul Klee. For almost a week he had dawdled with work. Around the house, Bonnie mostly ignored him. Sheila was spending long hours in planning sessions for Bonnie's empire. Binta was gone, off to New York to begin her new job. His brainchild, the Grand Odyssey needed attention, for which he didn't have the energy.

It seemed the only thing he hadn't lost was Chipper. Before Binta departed she had offered him one of her pups. Thinking that Chipper might not last long, George had accepted. Twice a day he went on long walks with Chipper and Maia, as he named the pup.

"What are you staring at?" Keys said as he walked into the office and plopped into a chair across from George.

Having no one else to talk with, George told his partner his plight.

"You're good with real estate and you've always been a good husband. But I could have told you you'd fuck up an affair."

"Oh?"

"You're not devious enough. Where do things stand with Bonnie?"

"No change except I'm sleeping in Tom's room. Not that she's home very much."

"Maybe you did her a favor giving her good reason to concentrate on her business."

"If she had turned up pregnant, I wouldn't have considered it a favor no matter how busy I was. How's Sunset Village going?"

"It's going. By the time it's built, it won't be worth much more than the debt. But a developer fee has kept food in the fridge. What's going on with your deal?"

George explained that the loan was scheduled to close in a couple of months, that River National Bank had gotten over the loss of Sears.

"You don't seem very excited. Do you want me to take over now that you've done the hard work."

"Very generous."

"Your mother could give you a job, Sport," Keys said with a smile and then a laugh.

"Who knows? Rather than make a lot of money on the Grand Odyssey, I might go to work for my 77-year-old mother as a barista."

Keys got up to leave, but added, "At least I made you laugh. Let me know if I can help."

George tried to jumpstart himself by making a to-do list. To-do lists had always energized him. They turned disorganized chaos into a sensible order. The list usually showed him that his life was full. Or full enough to distract him from difficulties. At the top of the list was to check in on how his mother was doing. If not a game changer from his present mental state, at least the visit would give him something to do.

At the shop, he took a turn making coffee drinks while the barista was on break. Stores at Mid County Mall had just opened and shoppers stopped by for a treat. "You're catching on," his mother said as he spooned foam into a cappuccino and she delivered croissants from the oven to the empty tray in the display case.

"Better not distract me or I'll be in trouble here," he said. Young baristas, often students with part-time jobs, received good, multi-task training for today's employment world. He marveled how a good barista read the orders, started one drink, poured one of four kinds of milk into a tin pitcher, heated the poured milk while starting the next drink, slowly poured the heated milk into the first drink, and then added whipped cream or a chocolate pattern on top of the foam. He didn't know whether to admire or feel sorry for them. "Debbie," he called out as he set the cappuccino on the counter.

"Oh no," Debbie said as she picked up her drink. She pointed behind him. He turned and saw his mother on the floor. Quickly he knelt beside her. She was unconscious. "Call 911," he shouted to Marie. He found a pulse and also a rapid, shallow breath. "Did you reach them?" Quick treatment could be critical.

While one EMT spread a stretcher, another quickly checked Helen Roth's pulse, breathing, blood pressure, oxygen level, and eyes.

"She has diabetes," George said.

"Start an IV," the first tech said. "She hit her head when she fell. Did she trip or faint? Did anyone see her fall?"

"She fainted," Debbie, the customer, said.

"Let's get her into the ambulance. We can draw blood there."

As they carried her, George asked, "Can I come with you?"

"Front seat if you want. We'll be too busy in back."

With siren blaring, they quickly drove onto the nearby highway and headed east to the teaching-hospital that wasn't far from the Arts District. George asked the driver what was going on with his mother, but she replied they'd have to wait for tests and a diagnosis at the hospital. Within what seemed like no more than 20 minutes from his mom fainting, they carried her into the emergency room. George followed as they rolled her into a small examining room.

Someone told him to sit in the corner while they did tests and treatment. This was his first experience in an emergency room since he was 9 and his mother brought him for stitches for a cut he got while crawling under a rusty barbed wire fence. The experience back then with medical staff sitting around and joking, half consoling-half teasing him about the mandatory tetanus shot, had no comparison to what he now watched. A heart monitor played a reassuring rhythm. Attendants wordlessly played their roles. Someone wheeled in a CT-Scanner. Someone else called attention to a screen showing the blood analysis from the ambulance draw.

"The doctor has a new emergency down the hall, but he'll be back to tell you what we know," said a nurse as shown on her nameplate. George thanked them, and drew his chair up to his mother's bed. She remained unconscious and had a bruise on her forehead.

Without thinking about the state of his marriage, he called Bonnie to tell her what happened. She raced out of a meeting and came to the hospital. She gave George a long hug, before sitting and staring at Helen Roth. "She seemed like she'd survive us both," she said.

"We didn't want to see this coming. I heard one of the staff comment about her standing up too quickly at the oven. Maybe fainted from low blood pressure."

"That happens to me so I get up slowly. What's her prognosis?"

"I don't know how I could have let her take over a coffee shop. "

"You couldn't have stopped her."

Bonnie was probably right. In fact he liked that he had helped his mom realize a wish, even a dream. She would never have accepted sitting around the house.

When the doctor returned he confirmed that the head injury was the major problem. "She's in a coma. We'll do tests to determine brain activity and whether she could recover. I'm not optimistic at her age. Within a week or two, she'll either wake up or go into a vegetative state, so it's pretty much wait and see. Does she have an Advanced Health Care Directive?"

George said he would bring it.

He recalled their lunch, almost a year ago, when she had asked, no demanded, that he not let her linger on science's latest devices. She had wondered whether he'd be willing to make the necessary decisions. Back then he had wondered also. Today, he knew he'd have to if she didn't recover.

George had read that someone in a coma could hear people talking. For much of the week he sat with his mom and talked about his memories from her life and how much she meant to him. He recalled her playing catch with him in the back yard after his dad had left for Viet Nam. One day in sixth grade the principal had caught him giving the finger to a friend and sent a letter home telling his mother to punish him. She read him the letter, laughed and said that was the dumbest thing she'd ever heard. "Just be careful who's around when you give the finger," she said. In the early 70s, she drove a '55 Chevy Bel Aire, "because of its pickup speed." She rarely cried after her diabetes diagnosis revived her desire for life, but she did at the death of Mr. Pitts, the mechanic who kept the Chevy running and with whom she had become close friends. He had taught her to change the oil and put in new sparks. He even tried to teach her to change the timing belt, but she finally sold the Chevy before a third belt was needed.

The coma affected Bonnie almost as much as George. She dropped by the hospital every day, even cancelled a trip to be around all week.

"Let's quit our jobs and run her croissant shop," she said

one day with tears in her eyes. "If she wakes up and goes home, my company can provide care around the clock at our house. We're hardly ever there these days except to sleep and maybe for dinner."

"I really appreciate your support," George said. He had told her and written to her how much he regretted causing her pain. And how much he admired and cared for her.

"We're a funny family," Bonnie said.

CHAPTER 37

Binta came home for a weekend to console George and to say goodbye to his mother with whom she had shared a balloon ride. George told about the drama, really melodrama, regarding Bonnie and Sheila.

"Welcome to the twenty-first century," Binta said. "One of my friends in the business school, an older woman is having an affair with a married man. The man's wife invited her to move in with them, and now the three of them live together. No ménage but she and the man still have sex, as do the man and the wife, and the wife has been trying out other men. Another friend invited me to join her group that parties and then everyone goes home with someone other than the person they came with."

"Sounds like the sixties."

"Your generation has affairs one at a time. By the way, how's Maia doing?"

"She's great. I love having her around. Chipper's hanging in."

One afternoon Sheila came by the hospital. "I adore your mom," she said. "That's you, I'm talking about," she said as she took his mom's hand.

"She likes you too," George said.

"George, do you have any male friends? All I see is a bunch of women. Bonnie, me, your partner, Binta, your mother. Turns out I'm having a son, and hope you know about dads and sons."

"How are you and Bonnie getting along."

"Just fine. She talks about you, says you've always been a square, and wonders how we ever got together."

"Not very flattering."

"She thinks I've changed you, loosened you up. Binta has also. Meanwhile she marvels at what she's accomplished. She still doesn't fully believe it. She says she's changed so much, she never knew this part of herself as a boss."

"I think it's always been there. She was a head surgical nurse. People don't expect women to start companies and soar to success."

"She claims she's not a feminist, but she's advanced feminism much more than anyone who merely talks about it."

Several weeks passed and the doctors said there was no hope for a recovery. Tom and Robin came home to see their grandmother one more time. They all gathered in her hospital room to share some memories and speak to her. Tom talked about his teaching job in Chicago, how his grandmother had taken him to the science museum and other museums when he was a kid, that because of those trips, he now has turned the aquarium and the Museum of Science and Industry into supplemental classrooms. He reminded his grandmother that she had encouraged him to become a teacher.

Robin said that she looked forward to graduating in June, that she wanted to be an active and caring person like her grandmother. She had talked with Bonnie about going to work in Bonnie's business in an administrative position and had talked with Seri McQuade about a similar job at the Family Planning Center. She thanked Grandma for having asked her to join her "croissant team." Neither of his children wanted to be a real estate developer.

Despite the vegetative state she had fallen into, Helen still retained her color as her heart continued to beat. She looked like she was taking a nap, which would make unplugging the breathing tube more difficult. George recalled how she had responded to her challenges and knew her nature was not to give up. He felt an urgency to keep his marriage together. He didn't know how, but he would try. And he would complete the Grand Odyssey though his heart wanted to take over the coffee shop.

The others said goodbye, one at a time. Tom brushed away tears. Robin said, "Thanks for being such a good grandma." Bonnie kissed her forehead and said thanks for all she had learned from her mother-in-law. George stayed behind to be there when the resident removed the breathing tube.

The others left and then Bonnie came back for a moment. "This isn't the time to figure out you and me," she said. "I'm happily stuck with this unimaginable run of my company. And will be for a while. It won't be forever, and I hope you're still around when I'm done so we can see if there's a life for us." They hugged, and he told her that he loved her.

While he waited, he remembered how his mother had eventually overcome the death of his father. One day she had walked into his room and said, "Let's go to the amusement park. I need a ride on the roller coaster." Scared the hell out of George as the train whipped around a curve and down a steep decline. When he had trouble in senior English, she read Moby Dick with him and discussed it every evening. He could do algebra while watching television, but he struggled to understand the meaning of the whiteness of the whale. It was his mother who prodded him to volunteer with the Family Planning Center. He never got over his worry for her after his father died. Despite her difficult challenges and regular risk-taking after her diabetes diagnosis, she never again gave him reason to worry about her mental state.

The resident walked in, nodded and handed some papers for George to sign to authorize removal of the breathing and feeding tubes. For the first time in his life, he heard what the resident described as the "death rattle," the total release of her final breath. She was no longer. George was an orphan. He remembered her explaining at a baseball game when he was 9 or 10, that the next hitter was waiting in the "on deck" circle. George was ready to step up to the plate.

Andy Greensfelder lives with his wife,
Jeanie Greensfelder, in San Luis Obispo, CA.

Made in the USA
Monee, IL
21 July 2021